PENGUIN CRIME FICTION

A COMEDY OF TERRORS

Michael Innes, in private life, is J. I. M. Stewart. Educated at Edinburgh Academy and Oriel College, Oxford, he has been Student of Christ Church, Oxford, and Reader in English Literature at the University of Oxford.

He has published many novels—including the quintet *A Staircase in Surrey*—and several volumes of short stories, as well as books of criticism and essays, under his own name. His *Eight Modern Writers* appears as the final volume in *The Oxford History of English Literature*. He is also the author of *Rudyard Kipling* and *Joseph Conrad*.

Under the pseudonym Michael Innes, Dr. Stewart has written broadcast scripts and many crime novels.

A COMEDY OF TERRORS

By

MICHAEL INNES

PENGUIN BOOKS

PENGUIN BOOKS
Viking Penguin Inc., 40 West 23rd Street,
New York, New York 10010, U.S.A.
Penguin Books Ltd, Harmondsworth,
Middlesex, England
Penguin Books Australia Ltd, Ringwood,
Victoria, Australia
Penguin Books Canada Limited, 2801 John Street,
Markham, Ontario, Canada L3R 1B4
Penguin Books (N.Z.) Ltd, 182–190 Wairau Road,
Auckland 10, New Zealand

First published in the United States of America by
Dodd, Mead and Company, Inc., 1940
Published in Penguin Books 1987

LIBRARY OF CONGRESS CATALOGING IN PUBLICATION DATA
Innes, Michael, 1906–
A comedy of terrors.
(Penguin crime fiction)
I. Title.
PR6037.T466C6 1987   823'.912   86-30255
ISBN 0 14 01.0090 3

Printed in the United States of America by
Offset Paperback Mfrs., Inc., Dallas, Pennsylvania
Set in Janson

A COMEDY
OF TERRORS

CHAPTER I

I HAVE seldom paid my annual visit to Basil without reflecting on the irrational nature of our feelings on birth and pedigree. Grandparents are, I suppose, necessary to an Englishman who would move in good society; great-grandparents are an advantage. But there the practical utility of ancestors stops. It has always been possible to make a gentleman in three generations; nowadays—when families are smaller and the upper class has to be recruited hastily—the thing is done in two. Nevertheless remote ancestors continue to be prized; the remoter they are the more proudly we regard them. And this is peculiarly illogical. Descent from our grandparents we share with only a few persons. But descent from any one ancestor in the reign, say, of John we share with virtually everyone in England. There is, in fact, sound elementary genetics behind the proposition that we are all sons of Adam. And this makes the pedigree business absurd. But what I am noting here is that it is a pleasant and stealing absurdity, and one which I have always felt come over me on going to stay at Belrive Priory.

My name is Arthur Ferryman. Pause over it and—if you are of the common visualising type—you will see a vaguely tattered fellow poking a flat-bottomed boat across a river. To this picture, however, you will have been betrayed by a false etymology; my ancestors gained their name by wielding a strikingly iron fist—*ferreus manus*—in the mediæval period. We are the slaves of words—writers particularly so—and I believe that this aristocratic derivation, together with the fact that at my private school I was called Punts, is responsible for much of my make-up. Lineage—

a successive title, long and dark,
Drawn from the mouldy rolls of Noah's ark—

can always fascinate me.

And so, more rationally, can the whole panorama of history. "O goodly usage of those antique times." Spenser expresses what is a profound secret conviction of mine. Fashionable contemporary novelist though I am, I believe the past to have been a far, far better thing than the present is. And Belrive, where the two toss uneasily in one narrow bed, quickens this antiquarian sentiment even more than it quickens the sentiment of birth.

Now the fascination of the past, according to psychologists, consists in its air of security. The past is over and done with; nothing more can happen in it; it is therefore a refuge from the difficult to-day and the problematical to-morrow. For me the Priory is the past; it symbolises an environment in which, to follow out this idea, one need not be perpetually braced to meet the shock of the unexpected. It may have been because I was relaxed in this way that the disaster at the Priory—so sudden and so unprepared for—bowled me over as it did.

A man likes to receive news of violence more or less impassively, and it looks as if an impulse to apologise in advance for my behaviour has made me approach my subject in a very roundabout way. I shall get more surely on the rails if I drop ancestry and the *hortus conclusus* of history and begin again with some account of the Priory itself.

Hortus conclusus. The Priory is that. For park, mansion and ruins are surrounded by a high wall—an early nineteenth-century wall which represents a last and costly protest against encroaching neighbours. When the Honourable John Byng toured the north of England in 1792 Cambrell and Wimms' cotton-mills were already rising hard by Belrive. Byng notes the deplorable fact that monks and cotton-manufacturers both need water, and that there is in consequence a tendency for the latter to spin where the former washed, meditated or fished. He notes too with disgust—it was a solitary tour and the future viscount when alone was inclined to gloomy judgments—the desuetude of agriculture round about and the sinister fact that the new industrial population is being fed from Liverpool on imported wheat. The mills have grown since the days of the Torrington Diaries but the same family still controls them; the Cambrell home—noted by Byng as a foolish overgrown citizen's box in the bad new taste—is now a mellow enough mansion on the outskirts of the town. The mills themselves, which dominate the Priory ruins to the south, are almost mellow by this time. A good part of Satan's kingdom is.

But quite new and staring is Cudbird's brewery, flanking the little park on the west. Brewers too need water; I understand that their wealth and curious social elevation arise from the fact that they need little else. Not that the Cudbirds are elevated. They are frankly plebeian. Horace Cudbird, a figure who comes into this narrative, I found it impossible to dislike. So, unfortunately, did Basil.

Belrive then, which centuries ago stood in a solitary valley up which opened a distant prospect of the Yorkshire dales, stands to-day—a plain anachronism—surrounded by a manufacturing town. A cotton-mill, a brewery, a high road: its triangle of territory is bounded by these. The high road, in my opinion, is the worst neighbour. It is true that the brewery smells. But until recently smells and civilisation have marched together; indeed, they do so to-day in some of the pleasantest places I know. It is true that the Cambrell mills have poisoned the fish—this despite numerous regulations on the whole, I believe, conscientiously observed. Still, with the mills has come the internal combustion engine, and with the aid of that one can make some of the finest fishing in the riding in just over half an hour. Mills and brewery yield to the high road, which has obsolete electric trams, buses, a constant stream of heavy industrial traffic, impatient business men twice a day in cars, impatient workers twice a day on bicycles, screaming children and shrill-voiced women from dawn to dusk—besides football fans in char-à-bancs, drunks, Salvation Army bands and electric drills at frequent intervals. I have always thought the trams particularly wanton; they charge along their indifferent track at a dangerous speed while the drivers thump steadily with their feet at harsh, cracked warning bells. A conductor has told me that they must keep to their time-tables or lose their jobs, and that this persevering malignant torture is the only way of avoiding imminent fatality every few score of yards; the existence of trams unsignalised by this horrid carillon would simply not be acknowledged by wayfarers. This may well be true. There are accidents enough as it is. The little lodge at the Priory gates is used so frequently as an emergency dressing station that the corporation might very reasonably be asked to pay a regular rent.

I am tempted to let this matter of the sheer noise by which the Priory is assaulted spill over into another long paragraph. There is, for instance, the curious fact that while the human inhabitants are most disturbed by those noises which are incessant the red deer in the park seem to be troubled only by special and occasional effects: the trams they ignore; the Salvation Army disturbs them; electric drills produce a panicky scattering most distressing to observe. But perhaps I have made my main effect heavily enough. The ruined Priory which yet speaks the quiet of the cloister, the Queen Anne mansion breathing the peace of the Augustans: these strangely environed by the clamour of our modern world.

The situation has its odd visual aspects as well. At night there is Cudbird's new neon sign. Standing on the terrace of the house one sees it just over the ruined tower. For a second there is darkness and the outline of the tower is barely visible against the dull glow of an urban sky. Then miraculously in the dark a great bottle leaps into being; this tilts itself like some crazy constellation in the heavens; a hundred flickering electric bulbs simulate the issuing beverage; the tower, cupped like a goblet below, receives the beery deluge. Thus does Horace Cudbird, a latter-day Ganymede, play cupbearer to his own obscure gods.

After dinner, guests unfamiliar with this spectacle will go out to the terrace and watch it for minutes on end. The thing has undeniably a certain bizarre beauty of its own. And down among the ruins Cudbird's sign produces more subtle effects. Here the monstrous bottle itself is invisible and one is aware only of a rhythmical succession of soft, reflected lights playing over the crumbling walls and amid the shadows. First comes the suggestion of an acid green—a skin of light which furs the massive masonry like an aura; the bottle has lit up. Next, rose-coloured shafts pass across the ruins like fingers up a keyboard; the city is being told in giant's lettering that Cudbird's Beers are Best. Suddenly the world lurches, wheels, circles; in a series of jerks the bottle is turning on its axis. And then a dull amber flood falls like a slow curtain; for a moment the Priory floats in a rippling sea of ale; then for seconds, and before the bottle again lights up, darkness reigns. It is in these seconds of inactivity, while Cudbird pauses between libations, that the effect is strangest. For in the darkness and by some trick of the retina these shadowy phenomena rapidly and confusedly repeat themselves; the mind is momentarily distracted between a flickering creation of its own and what it knows actually to lie immobile before it. A distinctly uncanny effect results. The Priory servants used to be fond of taking their sweethearts "to see the ruins"; since the sign went up it is in the other direction that one has to remember to walk at night if one would avoid embarrassing encounters.

This fiery flagon by night, the city's pall of smoke by day, the uproar which slackens only in the small hours of the morning: these make the setting, the foil, the frame for my cousin Basil's very beautiful home. The Ropers are artistically gifted—I acknowledge that it is from their side that I get such talent as I possess—and for generations they have applied to Belrive a taste which is conservative but never inert. As a result the place has that air of immemorial grooming which one associates with some of the great houses of England. The gardens are formal without being uneasily exotic; they do not, as some overwrought gardens do, call for other than a northern sky. The park is full of unobtrusive artifice, a margin illuminated in a hundred greens around the warm but sadly soot-stained stone of the ruins. The house in its exterior aspect is at once old and immaculate; it speaks of those two excellent things, continuity and a sound balance in the bank. Inside, one moves amid the blending and contrasting tastes of a succession of cultivated owners; there is that effect of a mild conflict of personalities within an acknowledged tradition which makes a house alive. In short, I find Belrive a most satisfactory place. And turning up the drive on the day this chronicle opens I found myself meditating, against the background I have now sketched, the slightly problematical figure of its master.

Basil Roper, the seventh baronet, was at this time a man in the middle fifties, a bachelor, famous, and just coming to the realisation that his career lay for the most part behind him. An explorer and mountaineer, he knew that never again would he stand so high above the sea as he had stood. At fifty one can climb to twenty thousand feet, perhaps to twenty-five thousand. Thereafter one's job is at the telescope and with the stores. The ultimate spires and pinnacles of earth will yield only to the faultless mechanism of a young man's heart.

Basil, like most climbers, had no single passion for altitude; he could get as much from the Central Gully on Lliwedd, a day's run from London, as he could from the traverse of some monstrous rock face in the Himalaya. Nevertheless the heart, as it has its tether as a piece of mechanism, has, as a principle of life, its goals. One of Basil's goals had been going very high indeed; the possibility had slipped away, and with it some tension which it was not perhaps easy to do without.

A man who has served an idea makes only an uneasy retreat upon practical affairs. But from youth Basil had been a scientist and he had his finger now in a number of pies—of those immaterial pies of the mind at which a man may stir to his heart's content, disturbing nobody and without fret or fuss. Into geological speculations he could step like a man entering the solitude of an arctic tent. To explore with a hammer among the rocks the barren æons of the earth gave him much the same satisfaction, I believe, as a physical vista of inviolate ice and untrodden snow. For such austerities I have myself small taste; I prefer the peopled earth—the field full of folk. Nevertheless I like to understand the ascetic type, and driving up Basil's avenue I made my yearly resolution:

to study my cousin once more with professional standards of assiduity. This perhaps has its own forbiddingly austere ring. But the imaginative writer is far from living on air. He has to apply himself to his fellows very much in the spirit in which Basil was wont to apply himself to archæan schists and eruptive rocks.

My taxi rounded a bend and the little park came into full view. It occurred to me what a remarkably valuable property it must be. Only the day before a friend had shown me a beautiful gold goblet recently excavated from some Viking hoard, an object of very considerable intrinsic worth which was yet far more precious in its character as a museum piece. Belrive was rather like that. Its position in the industrial district of a town by no means sufferng from stagnation or depression must surely render every acre worth a large sum of money; at the same time it possessed high value in another and indefinable currency, that of antiquarian or sentimental regard. I recollected that Basil's care of the Priory had always been scrupulous—but how strongly, I wondered, did he feel the responsibility of such a heritage? It came to me with something of a shock that my cousin cared nothing for the past. Or nothing for what I call the past. He would have been just the man to write that sort of outline of history which includes a great many illustrations of mammoths and pterodactyls and which relegates man to an appendix. Perhaps this sally is a little unfair. I realised that there was nothing vulgar or half-baked about Basil's historical sense. It was simply that human institutions of a sort with which we have any connection did not interest him. To certain remote and swarming cultures—Sumerians, Babylonians and the like—he gave, I believe, a sort of field naturalist's attention. But at the point where real history begins—the coming of the Dorian Greeks—his interest left off. And the chronology which really held his imagination and engaged his intellect was of the sort that reckons its years by the million. Just what value, I wondered, did Basil set on a twelfth-century ruin, or on ground which his ancestors had owned ever since they had successfully stolen it nearly three hundred years ago? The Tudor age must seem to Basil the merest yesterday. I glanced from my taxi and saw the iron skeleton of Cudbird's sign just dipping behind the Priory tower. To Basil these must appear virtually comtemporaneous constructions. And for the first time it occurred to me to speculate on the legal position in regard to Belrive. Was its owner entitled to do what he liked with it? Or were at least the ruins in some way protected from possible caprice?

These reflections were interrupted by a squeal of brakes and I was astounded to see Wilfred Foxcroft skipping hastily to the side of the drive.

Wilfred is a cousin of mine. Most of the people in this narrative are.

CHAPTER II

I WAS astounded to see Wilfred; I got a further shock when he turned towards me and waved what was distinguishably a revolver. The taxi drew up, and despite its doing so merely because I had tapped on the glass I could almost have believed myself involved in some incident of banditry. Wilfred opened the door, climbed in, and tossed his weapon carelessly on the seat. "I hope," I enquired, "that it isn't loaded?"

My cousin laughed, at the same time sitting down so heavily that I felt myself bounced towards the roof of the cab. "My dear Arthur," he said, "you understand the principle of the Verona drop?"

"Emphatically not."

"The Verona drop is a fragile bubble of glass which, under certain conditions, will resist a sharp blow with a hammer. What is called the safety catch on a rifle or revolver embodies just the same principle. A bump or jolt"—and Wilfred tossed the revolver to the floor—"merely increases the security with which the whole mechanism is locked."

Somewhat reassured, I reflected that Wilfred Foxcroft had not changed. Or his little habits had not changed. I remembered the jar against one's spine which that same slumping down on a hard bench at school could cause. From his schooldays too dated the irritating trick of accompanying every act of communication with some fragment of useless lore; he had the mental habits of an industrious but unimaginative squirrel and his head was a lumber-room of Verona drops and similar debris. I have sometimes thought that his quarrel with Basil— that enduring mountaineering quarrel which made me so surprised to see him at Belrive now—was not unconnected with this turn of mind. Wilfred's conversation was like an automatic machine: you dropped in some piece of conversational small coin and out came a dry biscuit—always virtually the same dry biscuit. And Basil's was perhaps rather like a comptometer: you pressed the keys and could rely on the relevant factual analysis taking place. The two tendencies came sufficiently close to each other to be mutually irritating. This irritation, exacerbated by enforced companionship and by privation, had been responsible as I always supposed for the rift. But here now was Wilfred back at the Priory and it would be decent to express my pleasure in the fact. I did this as simply as I could. "Wilfred," I said, "it is delightful to see you here again."

Wilfred tapped at the butt of the revolver with his foot until the barrel satisfied his sense of order by lying parallel to the driver's seat. "The suggestion of coming down," he said, "was a good one. A change at this time of the year is a capital thing. During the three winter months the incidence of common cold is nearly seven per cent lower in the provinces than in London."

I looked at him curiously. The statistics were of no interest to me, but my attention was held by the turn of phrase which had preceded them. *The suggestion of coming down was a good one.* Wilfred was perfectly capable of talking the King's English and this clumsy phrase was a deliberate ambiguity. Had the quarrel been made up on his initiative or on Basil's? It was impossible to say.

"Quite a family party," Wilfred was continuing. "Hubert and Geoffrey, Lucy, Cecil, Anne. I'm told that there are now only eight serious painters in England contriving to make more than four hundred a year. How lucky for you that people still buy books."

"Still *read* books," I corrected—taking an involuntary nibble at the biscuit as it shot from the machine. "Bankers, I suppose, are still in demand?"

Wilfred, a banker and a wealthy one, smiled complacently. "Hubert, of course, is doing well enough. The portrait commissions keep coming in. But Geoffrey, who hasn't at all followed in his father's tradition, doesn't make a penny. It's hard on that thwarted little tigress Anne. Do you know the price of a small prepared canvas?" And Wilfred, although devoid as I knew of any interest in the fine arts, proceeded to a detailed estimate of the working expenses of a painter. This monologue the reader will not expect me to report and I shall attempt instead to give some account of those relations whom I now knew I was to meet at the Priory.

I must be forgiven if I do not here work out a family tree; it is a writer's instinct to stick to prose, and in plain prose I think I can make everything clear. The eldest, then, of Basil's generation of Ropers had been his sister Margaret. She had married into the wealthy banking family of the Foxcrofts and had two sons, Wilfred and Cecil. Wilfred had gone into the banking business; Cecil,

whose bent was scholastic, was now the headmaster of a
public school. Both were unmarried, and both in age
within ten years of their uncle Basil.

Next to Margaret Roper had come Basil himself and a
year later there had been born Hubert, the painter.
Hubert's only child, Geoffrey, also a painter, was now
about twenty-five.

Youngest of Basil's generation was Lucy, now the
widow of a certain Charles Chigwidden, an unsuccessful
barrister. Lucy Chigwidden is a novelist: perhaps I may
be permitted to remind the reader that the term is an
elastic one.

I am myself the only son of Basil's aunt, Mary Roper;
my relationship to Basil, Hubert and Lucy is therefore
that of first cousin. Anne Grainger, the orphan daughter
and only child of my sister Jean, was now twenty-one.
Jean's marriage had been financially rash; she and her
husband were drowned in a yachting accident when
Anne was in infancy; the child had grown up under the
legal guardianship of Wilfred Foxcroft, whose protégé
she was now understood to be.

These paragraphs, I see, cannot pretend to be prose
after all. But they are clear and suit the artlessness which
this narrative must have; our exact cousinly relation-
ships—though these are scarcely relevant to what is to
come—may be worked out readily enough by anyone
who is interested.

We were now nearing the house and I interrupted
Wilfred to ask a question. "Hubert, Geoffrey, Lucy,
Cecil and Anne. Do I gather then that it is an unre-
lievedly family party?"

"Just that. A nice old-fashioned Christmas. I am to talk climbs with Basil; Hubert is to start on a portrait of Cecil; Geoffrey and Anne are to make love; and Lucy is going to pursue you into corners and elicit your views on the interior monologue and on chapterisation."

"Chapterisation?"

"Her new word. Why one begins a new chapter where one does." Wilfred chuckled at the involuntary sigh which must have escaped me. "When I come to think of it there is one outsider. Old Mervyn Wale."

"Sir Mervyn Wale," I said in surprise. "Surely he is the sort who never tears himself away from town and his expensive patients? And I didn't know he was any sort of family friend?"

"No more he is. But he and my brother Cecil have got uncommonly thick and Cecil seems to have persuaded Basil to ask him down. As for tearing himself away, he's looking distinctly ill and probably feels it necessary to ease off."

"At least," I said lightly, "someone who will stand outside the family passions."

It was not a tactful remark and I regretted it as I spoke. But Wilfred was not disturbed. "Wale, my dear Arthur, has no passions anyway. Only genuine scientific curiosity. Under the fashionable leech lies a real researcher—cardiac stuff, I believe. Or if he has a passion it seems to be for poor Cecil—who has certainly never inspired romantic devotion before."

I had no wish to listen to Wilfred disparaging his brother, a fault in breeding I had observed in him on previous occasions. I therefore changed the subject abruptly.

"The lethal weapon: what is the significance of that?"

For a moment Wilfred stared blankly. Then his eye went to the revolver. "Oh, that," he said. "As a matter of fact there are several. All the fun is to be with them."

"The fun?"

Wilfred rubbed his nose—a habit of his when about to open the lumber-room door. "Do you know," he said, "that the greatest number of pistol-duels engaged in by a single man is probably eighty-nine, a record achieved in 1889 by the Comte de Marsan—who was then, by a striking coincidence, just entering on his eighty-ninth year?" He paused. "Whereas with swords . . ."

Mercifully, our taxi jerked to a halt. I jumped out and glanced up the steps which led to the front door. Basil was at the top and waved as I began to climb. With sudden unreasoning dismay I saw that he had a revolver too.

Lucy Chigwidden was armed as well, but only with galley proofs. These were draped around her as she presided over Basil's tea table. Periodical grabs had to be made to disengage them from the cream cakes; they wrapped themselves round the admirable ankles of the parlourmaid bringing hot water and there was a moment of quintessentially English social embarrassment while they were a shade too deliberately retrieved by young Geoffrey Roper. Lucy had never had galleys before. They were the result of her present absorption in chapterisation. If one cannot quite bring oneself to decide where one's chapters leave off one need not expect pagedup proofs from one's publisher. Lucy appeared vaguely aware that at the changing dictates of her inspiration sweating men somewhere must break up and push about heavy masses of type-metal. Nevertheless inspiration must be obeyed. "Arthur," she said—and the spout of her teapot swayed alarmingly, like her own wavering mind—"*A single pistol-shot rang through the startled hall.* Would you say that that is too dramatic a note on which to break off?"

I experienced the uncomfortable feeling which always besets a writer when the actual and the imaginative seem to be mixing themselves up. The pistols were an established institution in Lucy's novels; now they appeared to be creeping uncomfortably out of her pages and into the hands of her relations. In a corner of the drawing-room Cecil Foxcroft was fiddling with yet another revolver.

"Really," I said, "it is difficult to tell; it depends so much on the key of your writing." I did my best to appear to be considering intelligently. "But it seems all right to me—most effective, indeed. *A single pistol-shot rang through the startled hall.* What could be more dramatic? There is a very similar effect somewhere in *Vanity Fair.*"

Lucy appeared pleased. I ventured to help myself to another cream cake.

"A single pistol-shot?" Geoffrey, the young painter, who was now sitting beside Anne Grainger in a window recess, spoke across the room. "What is the difference, Aunt Lucy, between a single pistol-shot and a pistol-shot?"

Lucy, although seeking literary criticism, had not

been seeking it on this sort of point. Chapterisation alone was in her head and this oblique attack disturbed her.

"And why"—I noticed that my niece Anne took her cue instantly from Geoffrey—"was the hall startled? Did the shot really ring through the startled hall, or did it ring through the hall and startle it?"

Geoffrey's father, Hubert Roper, who had been staring moodily into the great fire, turned round to his sister amid her litter of papers. "Did you say *rang*, Lucy? If the thing were out of doors, now, and in a frost, you might get just that sharp and clear acoustical effect. But in a hall I am not so sure. Have you tried it out?"

"After tea," said Anne, "we can go up to the gallery and fire a shot there. I'll put sixpence on the right word's being 'reverberated.'"

Basil, who was showing Sir Mervyn Wale a large map at a far end of the room, turned quickly round on this. I supposed that he was going to intervene in the baiting of his sister Lucy; it was, however, something else that was in his mind. "Certainly not, Anne. If this new amusement is to be safe there must be no shooting whatever except on the range. We had better make a rule that all ammunition is to be kept there under lock and key."

There was a murmur of approval, in which my own tones were certainly not among the least convinced. The revolver-shooting fad to which I had been so unexpectedly introduced appeared to me childish in itself and oddly "out" in the sort of house party characteristic of Belrive. I noticed that even Cecil Foxcroft, who affected the popular schoolmaster's zest for mechanical things, was handling the weapon he was examining gingerly enough. Why had Basil—if Basil it was—started such a craze?

Lucy had dropped more galleys and thrust her fountain-pen into a cream jug. "It shows," she said, "how careful one must be with adjectives. I mean, not to use them unless they are absolutely necessary." She glanced at me reproachfully, as if I had let her down in not being the first to chasten her style. "And do you think the pistol-shot had better 'sound'?"

"Unnecessary too," said Geoffrey. "Unless it had some impossibly effective silencer attached, of course it sounded."

Lucy considered, retrieved her pen, and began to write in what must have been a curious medium of cream and ink. "*There was*," she read aloud presently in a depressed voice, "*a pistol-shot in the hall.* I'm afraid I can't possibly end the chapter on *that*."

A moment's silence followed—a silence in which depression suddenly spread through the room. The badgering of Lucy made everyone conscious that the party was indeed a family affair.

It was the outsider, Sir Mervyn Wale, who attempted to deal with this uncomfortable pause. Haggard, old, with an eye withdrawn upon some inner labyrinth to which consumingly he must find the clue, he addressed us with professional smoothness from some outer surface of his mind. "I am sure," he said, "that Mrs. Chigwidden's pistol, whatever sound it may choose to make, will one day afford us much more of pleasurable excitement than any of the real weapons which are presently to be popping on Sir Basil's range."

The compliment—neat, if a shade too elaborately turned—fell upon people shifting uneasily in their seats. I suspected that Christmas at Belrive was not going to be a success.

CHAPTER III

IT WAS five o'clock and dusk was deepening to dark. In a corner of the room a mellow Dutch clock gave out the hour; the chime was cut on the fifth stroke by the swiftly rising and then sustained shriek of Cudbird's siren. And seconds later Cambrell's siren, as if indignant at being caught loitering, gave out a yet more piercing note. Others further away took up the chorus and for a minute the city might have been environed by a herd of unkindly monsters trumpeting in the advance of night.

"Why," asked Cecil Foxcroft, "should they not sound some pleasant-toned bell? It has always seemed to me that the siren, so peremptory and so unbeautiful, is as naked an expression of arrogance as could be conceived. Who would willingly be found addressing a fellow creature in tones corresponding to that brutal clamour?" And Cecil took off his glasses, raised his chin, and slowly surveyed the company. In just this impressive way, one supposed, was he accustomed to deliver himself of the right thing before his assembled school.

Cecil was a little over forty; his career had been brilliant; his status had always been well ahead of his age. This is not always a misfortune in learned walks of life. An able man can become, say, a fellow of an Oxford college at twenty-three and remain an agreeable twenty-three. But I suspect that it is almost impossible to become headmaster of a great school in the thirties and not grow into a bogus sixty-five at once. Cecil had been this sort of sixty-five for a good ten years. It was a capital impersonation; Cecil never ventured on anything he could not do well; only when the real thing was at hand for purposes of comparison could one detect the fiction. On this occasion Cecil had spoken just after the genuinely elderly Mervyn Wale. The effect was to leave a faint hint of mimicry hanging in the air.

"And yet," said Cecil—and one could imagine him now standing not before his pupils but before their parents—"I yield to no one in my admiration for the British industrialist. Take Ralph Cambrell. His hooter may be raucous but his heart is in the right place. How well he came out of the business of the new housing estates here. I am told he fought like a tiger for good-sized gardens and won the day."

"Ralph Cambrell controls Balltrop's," said Geoffrey.

"Balltrop's?" Cecil set his glasses suspiciously on his nose.

"The biggest seedsman," said Anne, "in the riding."

Again there was uncomfortable silence in the room, silence the quality of which was pointed by the steadily increasing rumble of traffic on the high road. From factories and offices in the city a thousand workers were pouring out to the suburbs, there to cultivate such of Balltrop's rathe primroses and periwinkles as the rigour of the season allowed.

Wale murmured something soothing about the legitimate interests of commerce. I spoke at random of the nerve-racking hubbub of a modern city and contrasted it with the pleasant human murmur which must have ruled in mediæval times. Wilfred took me up on this. "In Shakespeare's London," he announced, moving deliberately across the carpet towards the muffin-dish, "there were one hundred and fourteen churches, from the majority of which peals of bells rang intermittently throughout the day and night. In addition every shopkeeper employed a leathern-lunged lad to bawl his wares into the street." Wilfred paused with his muffin suspended in air, pleased with the alliterative quality of his phrase. "Arthur's golden age was really an age of iron and bronze, senselessly employed in a process of perpetual percussion."

Hubert Roper, tall and lounging, of a generation when artists still distinguished themselves by some trick of hair or dress, had extended his study of the fire to include Cecil sitting before it. "The midnight bell," he said, "who with his iron tongue and brazen mouth sounds on into the drowsy ear of night." He looked round as if inviting us to compare Wilfred's rhetoric with Shakespeare's. Then losing interest he turned again towards Cecil. It was the firelight on his nephew's glasses, I believe, which he felt to be important at that moment, and I remembered that there was some project of his making a portrait or sketch.

"Shakespeare's bells," said Lucy Chigwidden; "we must make a parlour game of them." Cheered by this happy idea, she bundled away her proofs. "Who can keep Shakespeare's bells ringing longest? And I begin. *Like sweet bells jangled, out of tune and harsh.*" She nodded to Wilfred Foxcroft.

Wilfred considered. "When Cecil speaks in that pro-

fessional way," he said, "'*tis like a chime a-mending.*"
He grinned at his brother.

It was my turn and I waved towards the windows and
the high road.

> "*The bells, in time of pestilence, ne'er made*
> *Like noise, or were in that perpetual motion.*"

Basil's voice came quietly from the big table where
he was still studying his map. "Not in Shakespeare,
Arthur." A moment's reflection told me that he was
right; I had recalled the lines from some other Eliza-
bethan dramatist. And here was something characteristic of Basil. Tucked away in his mind, so that I at least
had never been aware of it before, was a scholar's
knowledge of Shakespeare's text. Always from Basil
something wholly unexpected might come.

"Uncle Arthur is out because he cheated," said Anne.
It was lightly spoken; yet there was something hard in
her voice which I could not help resenting, and which
made the joke ill-mannered at the best. Lucy hastened to
continue the impromptu game. The search for bells in
Shakespeare ran round in a circle and came to Wilfred
once again. Basil had joined the rest of us now as a sort
of umpire.

Wilfred hesitated; Basil began to count ten slowly.
Suddenly Wilfred snapped his fingers.

> "*No longer mourn for me when I am dead*
> *Than you shall hear the surly sullen bell*
> *Give warning to the world that I am fled.*"

There was a pause; everybody, I think, was surprised
that Wilfred had survived a second round. And now

Lucy's laborious game took a somewhat gloomy turn. Most of the bells in Shakespeare—or most of those which we could remember—ring out upon some occasion of man's mortality. Geoffrey told us of *"sweet Helen's bells"*; Cecil cited *"a grief comparèd well To one sore sick that hears the passing-bell"*; Anne remembered *"a sullen bell Remembered tolling a departing friend."* And presently—for it was a game which even good and informed memories could not keep up for long—only Lucy and Wale were left.

It was Lucy's turn; she knitted her brows as Basil counted again. "No," she said, "I give in to Sir Mervyn." Her expression changed. "Stop! I can think of just one more: *My sighing breast shall be thy funeral bell.*" She glanced at Wale in triumph. *"My sighing breast,"* she repeated to him with emphasis, *"shall be thy funeral bell."*

Wale opened his mouth; then I saw him hesitate, his face curiously grim.

"Seven," said Basil, "eight . . ."

I glanced at Lucy, preparing childishly for triumph. "Nine . . ."

Wale raised his head. *"This sight of death,"* he said clearly, *"is as a bell That warns my old age to a sepulchre."*

His eye went round the company and rested for a moment on Cecil, who was fiddling again with the revolver which had been occupying him earlier. Rather awkwardly Lucy said, *"Romeo and Juliet*—of course." She had hardly done speaking when Wale turned abruptly and left the room.

We stared at each other uncomfortably. Then Geoffrey Roper stirred in his seat. "*A bell,*" he said, "*that warns his old age to a sepulchre.*" His face lit up. "By God, there's an idea for a picture in that!"

Oddly enough, dinner three hours later found everyone in excellent spirits. I say "oddly enough," and if I have succeeded in conveying something of the diffused uneasiness of the earlier meal the reader will understand me. Lucy's game had been obscurely distressing. It had also been pedantic. I have myself, of course, the professional writer's dislike of anything savouring of the literary competition, but I believe that the others too felt that searching one's head for stray lines of Shakespeare was rather a wantonly cultural amusement. It is significant that Basil's conversation at dinner, though unrelievedly learned, was far from giving any similar impression. Hyetal regions, mean annual cloudiness, co-tidal lines, cyclonic rotations and progressive low pressure systems are not charming in themselves. But Basil was fascinated by them and made them fascinating. My own attention, so perfunctory at first that I scarcely realised that this was the vocabulary no longer of geology but of meteorology, was completely held in the end. Nothing in the world is more boring than other people's hobbies— a proposition which I feared that revolver-shooting was amply to illustrate at Belrive. But meteorology, which must have been a mere hobby with Basil some years ago, was now plainly in another category. Basil had more than got it up; it presently emerged that he was discernibly pushing it along. He had recently formulated—and other people had proved—some theory which I understood only imperfectly, but which appeared to be a contribution of some little importance to what is a rapidly developing branch of scientific enquiry.

All this was impressive and said much for Basil's intellect. But more remarkable, and speaking for the power of personality which had made my cousin a great leader in organised mountaineering, was his ability to make this remote lore an instrument for bringing us together and raising our spirits. With the exception of Wale we were none of us scientifically inclined; we had some of us been at a dreary family loggerheads before we had spent half a day in the house. But now we listened and asked questions and understood. In a state of mild intoxication which had nothing to do with Belrive's excellent wines we even made suggestions which we fondly supposed might help. We were under the charm of a novelty made lucid by masterly exposition and stimulating by imaginative enthusiasm. Only Wale was a little aloof. But I could see that he was following closely and that he was impressed.

But of all this so luminous talk I retain, curiously enough, only the most general impression to-day. One aspect of the subject alone has stuck in my mind. Basil had a good deal to say about storm tracks, and on storm tracks I could still, I believe, write a tolerably full and accurate paragraph. There is a sort of tropical storm, it seems, which is next to unpredictable. Attempt to trace its causes and something seems to go wrong with the logic of the heavens; one is contemplating conditions which ought to lead not to storm but to calm. This alone I clearly remember, and I re-

member it because of its implicit irony. This talk of
Basil's had every appearance of bringing fair weather to
Belrive. Actually, it was a very cradle of the tempest by
which we were presently to be swept.

It was a fine night, dry under foot and frosty. After
coffee I put on a great-coat and strolled out to the terrace. Cecil was at a corner, studying Cudbird's vast sign.
He turned as I approached and it struck me that even in
solitude and the dark he would bend upon that fantastic
spectacle a glance carefully compounded of wise toler-
ance and inflexible judgment. "One must beware," he
said, "of applying to such things one's own rather chilly
standards of good taste. There is much vitality in them,
after all. Shelley would have delighted in that bottle."

If there was anybody, I reflected, at whose hypotheti-
cal reactions it was futile to guess, Shelley was the man.
I made a noncommittal murmur.

"Or take Lucy's stories," Cecil went on. "Doubtless
they seem extravagant and crude enough to a disciple of
Henry James." At this Cecil tapped me on the shoulder
—an action which I must confess stirred me to obscure
resentment. There is in James, heaven knows, ten times
more than I could ever hope to learn: nevertheless I am
beyond the age at which one relishes being pigeon-holed
as the disciple of this man or that. "And yet, my dear
Arthur, Lucy's romances provide a great deal of innocent diversion. Moreover it is diversion with what may
fairly be called an intellectual appeal, and this is an es-
timable thing in an age so recklessly emotional as ours."
Cecil took off his glasses. "Some of us, I fear, lead sadly

ill-regulated lives to-day."

It was at this point that I realised that Cecil was up to something, and that Shelley, James, Lucy and her books had served to introduce a general proposition which was in its turn to be illustrated by some particular instance. "Ill-regulated lives?" I asked. Whatever the confidence might be, it might as well be got over.

Cecil took me by the arm; the action might have been described as his house-master's grip. "Our walk," he said, "shall be to the ruins."

It was half-past ten when we got back and I had resolved to go straight up to bed. Passing through the drawing-room I found Basil again bent over his great map. Hubert was lounging beside him, a considering eye bent not on the great square of cloth but on his brother. I stopped with the intention of discovering what quarter of the earth was under review. But something intent about both men made me pass on without disturbing them. All I heard was fragments of what appeared to be a new vocabulary that evening: the Ross Quadrant, the Victoria Quadrant, the Barrier.

The words meant nothing to my waking mind. But in sleep I knew better. I dreamt that night of a great waste of snow, of snow everywhere stretching to a remote horizon. I dreamt of Basil environed by this, absorbed, alone, his map before him on a table of ice. I dreamt of my niece Anne Grainger holding a revolver and saying in a hard voice: "Uncle Arthur is shot because he cheated. Uncle Arthur is shot."

CHAPTER IV

"Shooting this morning."

Wilfred Foxcroft, investigating the breakfast kidneys, pronounced the words with an emphasis which made me start. His brother Cecil, who was addressing himself —characteristically as I thought—to a boiled egg, looked up equally sharply. "Will that not keep," he asked, "till the afternoon? This is a holiday reunion, no doubt. But I have an idea that there is urgent family business to consider nevertheless."

Wilfred shook his head. "Family business—particularly if it is urgent—is always better put off." He smiled happily at this witticism, which struck me as more salted with truth than much of Cecil's more measured wisdom. "Basil and I once discussed family affairs at twenty-two thousand feet—with deplorable results."

Everybody was startled. The party at Belrive was indeed a holiday reunion, but it was also—evidently— an occasion of reconciliation. An old quarrel, of which the cause was surely obscure to all but two of those present, was being made up. Basil and Wilfred had come together. The last thing to be expected was that one of them should now begin to air the past. We were all slightly shocked, therefore, at Wilfred's remark; at the same time we all hoped, of course, to hear more. Ten years ago these two men, uncle and nephew, had disappeared up a mountain with a small band of porters—the

two of them thick as thieves. They had come down again
hazardously by different routes and with a hastily divided
commissariat. A month later they had met in Darjeeling
and in silence shaken hands in the presence of friends.
When the breach had occurred they had been not individuals merely but climbers belonging to a famous club;
they complied with a form; they did not meet again. That
was the story. And now here was Wilfred seemingly prepared to babble about it.

But he was only tantalising us. "The quarrelsome altitude," he said. "Another three thousand feet and one
would view with only the most lackadaisical disapproval
one's dearest enemy in the world. Particularly if one
were at all ahead of one's acclimatisation. I don't know
what are Wale's views, but I believe myself that an in-
crease in the hæmoglobin of the blood—" And Wilfred
was off on one of his instructive harangues.

Basil watched him—I thought with a slightly narrowed
eye—and interrupted on the first pause. "To go back to
Cecil's point," he said gravely, "there really is, I believe,
business for some of us." He was choosing his words
with evident care. "Family business may be tedious, and
it is often sound doctrine to let it settle itself, no doubt.
But there are times when a person is entitled to formal
dealing and to expedition. I do urge that."

Hubert Roper put down his cup. "Urge it?" he said.
"More than that. You exemplify it."

I had an inkling of what Basil was at; I remembered
my conversation with Cecil on our stroll the night before. Hubert's words, however—or rather their tone—
baffled me; they had an enigmatic quality which might

have commended them to Lucy. But Lucy, I fear, though listening was not listening in the right way. It is all a matter of ear, the writing of novels.

"Formal dealing?" said Wilfred, taking up Basil's phrase. "Rather a portentous expression, surely. And I really don't know that we need hurry. Geoffrey, I am sure you are on my side."

Was this malice or good humour? I had to admit that I could not listen delicately enough now myself. Geoffrey, in his invariable place beside Anne, was voting for good humour—perhaps as a matter of policy. "Oh, certainly," he said. "Why should you hurry, after all? All that is for the young."

"And what interest," asked Anne, "has my guardian Wilfred in the young? None at all, I hope."

Malice or good humour—I could not tell. My ear assured me only that Anne and Wilfred understood each other. But of how that understanding had come, or what attitudes and emotions it comprehended, I knew nothing. A struggle that was almost deadly; a tussle of wills that was finally friendly enough: either of these things might be. Cecil, of course, was a witness to the state of affairs. But that he was a reliable witness I was not convinced. Nothing was obvious except that Anne and Geoffrey were in love; that neither had a penny; and that Wilfred was implicated in their future. This and that Basil was trying to take a hand. Why? Though actually Wilfred's uncle, he was very little in a position of seniority, and his relationship to Anne was distant—much more distant than my own. What, in the whole complexion of family affairs, could be making him specially anxious to see the young people's future straightened out? And what, once again, had made Hubert, the heir to Belrive, say in that peculiarly charged way that in the transacting of family business Basil exemplified formal dealing and expedition? It was meditating this question that made me first really uneasy as to what was going forward at the Priory.

Sir Mervyn Wale enquired for marmalade—so smoothly that there was an immediate embarrassed recognition that this was not, after all, exclusively a family gathering. It was curious, if delicate negotiations were really on foot, that this eminent stranger should have been invited down. I remembered, without much illumination, Wilfred's statement that Wale was here at the instance of Cecil, with whom he had struck up a close friendship. So far I had been unable to discover what interests these two had in common. Wale was a physician; Cecil was a classical scholar. I wondered if Wale was perhaps an influential governor of Cecil's school.

At the moment family matters were abruptly dropped. Talk turned to the revolver-practice and I began to get a hang of what had happened. Somewhere in the ruins Basil had built himself a range as an outdoor amusement on winter days. I could hardly imagine why, but this was no doubt because, like Lucy, I regarded pistols as slightly sinister weapons. Basil, apparently, was something of an expert, and the sport does not require the space and the elaborate precautions necessary for a rifle range. Until its novelty waned in a few days' time the pistols were clearly to be all the go; I came to the conclusion that it would be only sociable to take an interest in them myself. There was a good deal of fun now directed at Lucy Chigwidden on the sufficiently obvious theme of her practical ignorance of firearms as contrasted with the prominence accorded them in her violent narratives. All this Lucy took in very good part; light on the subject of chapterisation had come to her in bed and she was in equable spirits. . . . And then Geoffrey asked his uncle if anyone was coming to the shooting from outside.

Basil regarded us with just those narrowed eyes which he had been directing on Wilfred a little before; his glance was accompanied by what was rare with him indeed: a faintly satirical smile.

"Why, yes," he said. "Horace Cudbird is sure to come."

There was a little pause in which one heard cups, knives and forks being put down abruptly. Cecil was the first to speak. "Cudbird? Really, Basil, I should hardly have imagined . . ."

"Let us study," said Geoffrey, "Cousin Cecil yielding to no one in his admiration for the British industrialist."

"But at the same time," said Anne, "drawing the line."

"Endeavouring rather," said Geoffrey, "to draw Uncle Basil's line."

"Let us hope, rather, that he draws his fire."

"Has Uncle Basil fire? Or only ice?"

There was a good deal of laughter, in which I did my best to join. For this piece of cross-talk was aimed at me; it represents a parody—not, I hope, a sufficient one—of the sort of dialogue I have been developing in recent years. My attention was held by the final play on ice;

it reminded me of Basil amid that arctic waste in my dream. Could my cousin be proposing to engage in some form of polar exploration? Perhaps Geoffrey's implication had merely been of something finally cold in Basil's temper.

"Are we to see Ralph Cambrell this time?" Wilfred asked. "He has always seemed a good fellow to me."

"Cambrell? Yes, he is coming to lunch. We have something to settle together." Basil spoke distinctly without enthusiasm. "Cudbird is a man of ideas."

We knew that Basil rarely threw out gratuitous commendations, and I remembered that quite recently he had taken a severe view of the setting up of the brewery's big electric sign. Everybody seemed to feel that in what he had said there was food for thought. A good deal of coffee was consumed in silence before Geoffrey said: "Anyone else?"

Basil nodded. "Mr. X."

We stared at him.

"I cannot," said Basil with mocking seriousness, "tell you more. Except this: for one of you Mr. X is a special treat. And he will be here for dinner."

I do not think that my walk that morning was much disturbed by the mysterious currents which were beginning to stir in my cousin's house party. A powdering of snow had fallen and in the park the trees, bare and soot-begrimed, showed like frozen fountains of ebony. Everywhere the eye saw silence; the hubbub from without, itself something diminished at this hour, was doubly an invasion and a wrong: against it a single hidden storm cock, the missel thrush of the north, sang a clear defiant strain. A gardener's boy, breaking off from the satisfied contemplation of frost on his recently dug beds, trundled his barrow over to greet me; I had known his father and could just remember his grandfather too.

I felt at home. Many of my school holidays had been spent at Belrive; indeed, it was the nearest thing to a fixed centre that I had known. My father was an engineer, frequently occupied in South America; his passion was for the continent of Europe and when not constructing bridges in Brazil he would be prowling with a Baedeker through the streets of Bonn or arguing with a courier on the best route from Modena to Montagnana. And like many prosperous Englishmen of his day he thought it the natural thing to travel *en famille:* nurses, governesses, tutors succeeding each other with the years. My schooling was perfunctory; my early impressions are all of a Europe in ceaseless motion: the rock and olive of the Dalmatian coast heaving past the deck of a foul-smelling Greek steamer out of Trieste; Holland flowing smoothly across the windows of a Pullman car and a scuffling excitement to observe, running along a dyke, the incredible novelty of an electric tram; the vineyards of the Viennese hills circling slowly as a carriage laboriously climbed—beside me an elderly Englishwoman, fortuitously met, extracting water-colour sketches from a portfolio to show my mother. As an education it was incomparable; by seventeen I had acquired what every novelist would beg of the gods: a tolerably intimate knowledge of three capitals. I don't know that Scheherazade herself had more.

But as a way of life it had not conduced to the formation of any local piety and I would have grown up wholly rootless but for Belrive. A villa at Ventimiglia or San Remo, a flat in Paris, a London club as jumping-off ground for the houses of acquaintances discreetly cultivated: from just that Belrive had, I suppose, swung me away. It had given me a taste for ground of my own; it was the reason of my possessing to-day a solid house in Chelsea, pleasantly cluttered with the accumulated possessions of years. This meditation, pursued as I strolled now over snow and now over crisply frosted grass, did not make me less pleased with my surroundings. In the solitude which one could gain in Belrive's little park there was something peculiarly attractive. So strangely secluded from the city, the place had the quality of all unlikely retreats: the hollow to which one can sometimes clamber behind a waterfall, a cave which delivers one unexpectedly from the beat and the glitter of the sea. I was slightly annoyed when, on turning the corner of an isolated shrubbery, I came upon Cecil and Mervyn Wale.

They had brushed the light snow from an upturned cattle-trough and were perched in somewhat uneasy dignity on the resulting low seat. I noticed a robin perched on a twig hard by—and it was the robin which made me pause as I was about to advance upon them. For the bird struck me as viewing the scene with the inquisitive and considering air of its kind; it seemed to be asking itself what was going forward; and a mysterious sympathy prompted me to do the same. For a moment I stayed my steps, and in that moment an odd conviction came upon me. I was about to interrupt a professional consultation.

If Cecil had been thrusting out his tongue or Wale manipulating a stethoscope I could not have been more convinced—though actually the two men were only conversing earnestly together. It must have been Cecil who gave the thing away. He was something of a *poseur* and a little more than slightly self-important; his type is not at its ease when consulting inscrutable fate in the guise of a Harley Street medico. I paused awkwardly, very much as if by some mistake of a nurse or servant I had been ushered into a consulting room where another patient was being palpated on a couch.

The robin, as if satisfied with having occasioned this fatal hesitation, whisked its tail and flew away. In the same moment I realised that I had not been observed, and thought good to follow its example. Retreating behind the shrubbery, I glanced round for some other route which I might take. As I did so I wondered if here was the reason for Wale's being at Belrive. Could Cecil, unbeknown to us all, be so confirmed a valetudinarian that he must have a trusted doctor with him wherever he went? It seemed almost impossible. Without much knowledge of the economics of the medical profession, I could yet guess that to retain Wale in such a way would be to face an almost astronomical bill.

My speculations—which were those of the merest busybody, I must confess—were abrupted by two quick reports from the direction of the ruins. The pistol-shooting was beginning. With some thought of going in that direction I turned half round and saw Cecil moving off

alone across the park. The consultation—if consultation
it had been—was over. I went on my previous way.

Wale was still sitting on the trough, a shrunken and
curiously concentrated figure. And once more I made
that awkward pause. Solitary though he was, there
seemed yet something I was loath to interrupt. He was
looking after Cecil; his face was in little more than pro-
file; there was no mistaking his expression, nevertheless.

Or there ought to have been none. For just that expression I had seen and marked before. As I advanced
upon him now—for it was impossible to skulk longer at
the bidding of these fugitive impressions—I reflected that
if only I could recall on whom and upon what occasion
I had remarked it in the past I should know something
odd about Sir Mervyn Wale.

CHAPTER V

THE DUTCH and Flemish artists painted sitting on a stool; the Italian Old Masters painted standing. I have noticed that a majority of modern painters of my acquaintance follow the Italian habit, and I believe this has been general since the time of the Impressionists. The painter stands before his canvas, retreats from it backwards like a courtier before royalty, contemplates his subject, advances rapidly, strikes at the canvas and again retreats. Young Geoffrey Roper, I knew, painted like this. And this is why I was surprised that he was such a bad shot. A man who could bear swiftly down upon an easel and flick a splash or speck of pigment just where it was wanted might reasonably be expected to make a better show as a marksman than Geoffrey was contriving on his uncle Basil's range.

At the beginning I was next to hopeless myself. With a shot-gun I can acquit myself just below mediocrity; my efforts raise friendly ridicule in others, but not the embarrassment which attends going out with a positive duffer. A revolver was an unfamiliar weapon and, I felt, a futile one. If one is inexpert one has to stand so near the target that it is difficult not to feel that it would be altogether simpler to step up to it and use one's fists. And I doubt if I should have attempted to improve had it not been for Wilfred.

Wilfred abundantly entertained us with what may be

termed the lore of the revolver: its evolution from a
primitive form, its mechanisms, the ballistic laws involved. To escape this I concentrated on marksmanship
and as the morning's rather desultory sport wore on I
found myself making progress. But Geoffrey, if anything, seemed less proficient than at the start. At eight
paces he was unable to put two bullets within a foot of
each other. Anne was laughing at him and this—perhaps
because their alliance was commonly unflagging and directed upon every trifle—he seemed not to like. He continued to take part with a sort of scornful irritation infinitely shocking, I don't doubt, to those who cherished
orthodox attitudes to sport.

And among these, inevitably, was Cecil. Cecil had
taken upon himself what I thought of as his touch-like
pose. Just so would he stand on his playing fields, en-
couraging (at a sort of modified shout, which ingeniously
consulted both dignity and vehemence) the muddy ma-
nœuvrings of his pupils. He had never himself stepped on
a rugger field in his life; I could remember him, on the
strength of a weak heart, spending most of his afternoons
in the school library. But it would have been difficult to
guess this of the headmaster who was so keen on the
game. Or difficult for all but schoolboys. Wilfred had
told me how Cecil was found out. He had for some fatal
weeks failed to master the significance of the shout, "All
on." This, apparently a technical term connected with
the off-side rule, Cecil had carelessly taken for granted
as an exclamation of simple encouragement. He had used
it as that—to the horror of the school, so that the thing
became a legend. The mistake was, one can guess, an

uneasy memory in Cecil's mind. But here he was in his best athletic impersonation, exclaiming "By Jove!" with manly vehemence and "Oh, good shot!" as if a bull's-eye was the rational passport to his extreme regard.

"Cousin Cecil is ardent," Anne said.

"He relaxes the bow," said Geoffrey. "He pulls the trigger. He encourages the warriors. He calls upon the gods. And presently, surely, he will distribute the prizes."

"But Cousin Wilfred distributes marks. There is emphasis on good conduct and second in importance is general knowledge. A prize may conceivably follow at the end of the year."

They were at it again. Cecil and Wilfred were out of earshot; the parody was for my benefit alone. I realised that they had been reading my last book, *The Kinsmen*—having borrowed, no doubt, the copy I had sent to Basil. The reiterated mockery irritated me; perhaps it was because of this that I suddenly saw these two as a couple of precious spongers. They were quite frankly out to extract money—an income, a settlement or whatever it might be—from Wilfred. And they thought to veil the social indecency of this attitude behind a screen of sophisticated talk. At the moment *my* talk. I turned to Anne. "Are you sure," I asked, "that you are conducting your operations in quite the right way?"

I ought not to have intervened; it was no business of mine. Basically, too, my sympathies were on their side. As a painter Geoffrey had a real line, and he was sticking to it. I had myself once stuck to a sort of fiction in which a year's work brought in forty pounds; if it came to a little moral pressure on a wealthy relative I was far

from wanting to disapprove. And Anne too was a hope-
lessly uneconomic proposition: intellectual, odd, a re-
viewer of little volumes of verse nobody else read. Could
she at a pinch boil an egg? I doubted it. Most injudiciously, she had been brought up in an environment in
which ringing the bell for eggs is part of the law of
nature. They were nature's own spongers, inconsiderable
members of a class which sweetens life with imagination.
I repeated my question with a more friendly intonation.

Anne laughed. "Wilfred," she said, "is going to gather
his dependents round the death-bed. And then how infinitely charitable he will be."

Geoffrey stared at her reflectively and nodded. "He
will keep only the *Encyclopædia Britannica*. In that he
will read his own last offices and hope to retain a good
deal of information that they have long forgotten in
heaven."

"May I, Sir, recall an interesting fact about the throne
on which You are at present seated?" Anne had put her
hands together as if in prayer. "It is equally compounded
of chrysoprase, chrysoberyl, beryl and chrysolite, and it
was constructed to an original design by Moloch himself."

A pistol banged. There was no sense to be got out of
them. But Anne was my niece and I tried once more,
turning to Geoffrey. "But aren't you being rather impatient? And are there not other ways of arranging things?
Surely your father, who has such solid expectations . . ."

Geoffrey jerked his head backwards. "Look at my
father now."

I looked. Hubert Roper was standing a little removed

from the shooting, staring back at the house. He was in a brown study; about his whole attitude there was something extraordinarily sombre.

"And look," continued Geoffrey as if continuing an argument, "at Horace Cudbird."

I turned round. Advancing across the frosted grass was a small stout smiling man in a new, very cheap suit. Between the banging pistols one could hear the loud creak of his boots. This was indeed Horace Cudbird, the wealthiest man in the town.

"Ferryman?" Cudbird said to me when we were introduced. "You're one of the family though. I can tell that." And he glanced first at Basil and then back at myself with brisk appraisement. I got the impression that my cousin and I might be two tubs of malt or loads of hops. "Canaries are wonderful for sharpening the eye that way."

The shooting had been interrupted and a little circle had formed for the purpose of introductions. Cudbird looked round it in the most friendly fashion and continued to talk. "For following out a strain of blood ther's nothing like practice on canaries. And I've kept them, Sir Basil, for as long as I can remember now. And kept notes on the breeding of them. And a funny thing happened about that."

We made polite murmurs.

"It came of my lad's wanting an electric train. He was saving up for that and he thought: 'Why not get hold of Dad's notes on the canaries and send them to the *Fancier?*' It won't be known to you, but you can guess that's a paper for those that keep birds."

Cudbird paused. I realised that in the trivial anecdote which was going forward we were all oddly prepared to be interested.

"And send them the nipper did. A few weeks later they were printed, and there was a couple of guineas more towards the train."

Cudbird had produced a very old pipe. He stopped to begin a cleaning operation—obviously a simple rhetorical wile to achieve suspense.

"And the next thing was a professor from Cambridge, with the *Fancier* in his pocket, ringing the door-bell and chasing me from home to the office. We got in one of the stenographers and spent a morning putting down everything about canaries I ever knew."

There was a genuinely impressed silence. I think we were chiefly struck by the realisation that the man was not bragging. It was his imagination, not his pride, that had been engaged by this incident. That he and the professor from Cambridge should have got together over canaries was natural; the oddity consisted in the way it had happened.

"It's curious," continued Cudbird, becoming metaphysical and confirming this interpretation, "how one thing does follow on another. You never know"—he raised his head and his eye left us to sweep round the ruins—"what your ball won't set rolling. That talk with the professor meant a contribution to genetics—a thing I'd scarcely thought of before, though I've read about it since a fair amount. And it would never have happened"—his eye returned to us humorously or ironically

—"if Jim Meech hadn't thought to deliver potatoes. . . . But, Sir Basil, you'll want to be getting on with the morning's sport."

Some of us undoubtedly wanted to employ ourselves that way. And I myself had another preoccupation; I was beginning to feel the need for reflection on a number of things which had happened at the Priory since my arrival. Nevertheless I was pleased—as were, I think, the others—when Wale said with suave encouragement: "I feel a good deal of curiosity, Mr. Cudbird, about Jim Meech." Nobody could have been less like Coleridge's Ancient Mariner than this prosperous, cheerfully plebeian but by no means vulgar little brewer. But he had something very like the Mariner's trick. He commanded attention. Any amount of pistol-popping would have been as powerless upon us as was, upon the wedding guest, the loud bassoon.

"When I was a lad I always wanted canaries. Not just one canary but a little aviary of them, so that I could watch how they behaved. The question was how to get them; there wasn't any money, of course." Again we got a slightly ironical glance.

"Down at the lower end of the market, where you go in by Stonegate, there was a fellow who sold them; I watched him for a time and saw he didn't sell any too many. I made a bargain with him. For every ten canaries I sold for him I was to have one for myself. I think now I could have got him down to one for every five—but of course in those days I didn't well know my way about at that sort of thing."

Basil, who was clearly pleased with Horace Cudbird,

gave a rare chuckle. "I dare say you've learnt since."

"Yes, Sir Basil, I have. We all must, unless . . ." His eyes flickered disconcertingly towards Geoffrey Roper, who did contrive to give rather obviously an impression of being one of the lilies of the field. He broke off. "But now the question was: how to sell any more canaries than the fellow was already selling himself? It was then I heard about Jim Meech having started to deliver his potatoes. Jim had a vegetable stall hard by and he'd seen what heavy baskets the women had by the time their marketing was over. It occurred to him he might make pretty well a corner in potatoes—about the heaviest thing —if he'd undertake to deliver them, just as if he had a shop. So he took orders and when market was over out he'd get the donkey and round he'd go. It was hard work but it did the trick."

"Mr. Meech too," said Cecil, a little too graciously, "was of the learning sort."

"No doubt. Well, I took on Jim's deliveries—for nought." Cudbird paused and looked at Cecil. "For nothing, that is to say."

I was pleased to see Cecil slightly confused. Cudbird, friendly though he was, had all his defences in order.

"And so I got to know the womenfolk in all that part of the town. I'd hear if their men were in work and what they were making, and I'd hear about their kids and I'd give them a bit of a ride in the donkey-cart by turns. I borrowed a cap."

"A cap?" said Anne.

"Yes, Miss Grainger. I borrowed a cap from some other lad who was made to wear one and didn't like it.

And then I'd walk about those streets in my spare time as if I was on an errand and whenever one of the women-folk went by I'd touch it in a shy sort of way as if I'd taken a particular liking to her. Like a lad going about in search of a second mother. And then I went to work at the canary stall. The women would come to Jim's for their potatoes and see me on my new job and they'd come over for a word. In a couple of months I had four canaries of my own."

"And now," said Basil, "you have the world's biggest and brightest bottle." He spoke without rancour.

Horace Cudbird nodded gravely. "That may be," he said. "But the brewery can never mean to me what those four canaries did. They were a start." He turned to me. "Like the first manuscript that didn't come back from the publishers, Mr. Ferryman."

Here was a man very aware of the world. There was a silence. Cudbird stepped back and again surveyed Belrive. "You never can tell," he said in his former gnomic manner, "what will come of an idea."

CHAPTER VI

I AM discovering that a narrative of this sort presents
technical difficulties of a sort which would not confront
me were I writing a novel. The discovery is interesting;
I feel like turning back and writing a Jamesian preface
on the problems of a romancer turned chronicler. But
what reader wouldn't skip anything of the sort? I had
better go straight ahead.

One difficulty, though, may be noted down. At this
preliminary stage—which is, at least, now nearly over—
one has to marshal a number of incidents and individuals
the significant connection between which and whom
may, if logic is to be preserved, only appear later. Of
these relations of mine of whom I am writing I doubt if
there is a single one of whom I have not by this time had
to record some more or less cryptic remark. And though
the cryptic is beguiling in moderation it can very quickly
become boring. Sir Mervyn Wale, for instance, quotes
Shakespeare in an obscurely significant way—and well
and good. But when all these other people begin to
spread themselves in much the same fashion the reader
may well come to feel that it is a little tiresome. Working
as a novelist I should so twist my facts as to enable me
to cut down this element to that judicious proportion at
which it is a spur to interest. But here the facts are given
me by God—or by the Devil, maybe. I simply have to go
on recording what appear to be disjointed incidents until

I am out of the wood. And I am nearly out now. Still,
a number of things have their place before the catastro-
phe. How Ralph Cambrell, the cotton spinner, joined in
the shooting after all; how he had an embarrassingly public quarrel with Basil; how Hubert Roper set about his
nephew Cecil's portrait; how Basil kept up his joke about
the mysterious Mr. X who was coming to dinner: these
seem to be the chief remaining elements of the prologue.
Over them I promise not to waste the professional writer's too-ready ink.

I had met Cambrell before. Being unable, like Cecil,
to endow individuals with vague characteristics in terms
of their occupations and interests—not believing, in fact,
in an abstracton called the British industrialist—I was able
to judge him for what I thought he was. And I thought
of Ralph Cambrell as a smooth scoundrel.

The emphasis must be on *smooth*. He was more obviously this than scoundrel. But, again, it was of his mind
only that smoothness was a characteristic. It would be
wholly misleading to suggest that he had an oily—or even
a particularly supple—manner. His manner was direct
and covered mental processes which were instinctively
oblique: of this obliqueness I take the business of Balltrop's seeds and the housing estates to have been characteristic—the profits not so substantial as the intrigue
pleasurable in itself. Perhaps I was too ready to judge
the man unfavourably. He was a gentleman—an abstraction, this, which means something to my way of thinking—and I have a prejudice (in England at least three
centuries out of date) against gentlemen giving them-

selves wholly to huckstering, money-changing and what the Victorians called the progress of manufactures. It is not in the least my position that these activities are beyond the pale. But a man brought up liberally and to a position of privilege should be able to tuck them away. Wilfred, to do him justice, could do this; he could disentangle ends and means; he understood leisure. Cambrell, on the other hand, I felt lived in his mills; he carried them about with him; when he presented himself as concerned with anything else that something else was a fraud—and a fraud undertaken in the interest of some ulterior commercial design.

All this was rather more than I really knew about the man. I had him typed that way. But I found myself, as he strode across the grass towards us now during the revolver practice, involuntarily taking this train of thought a step further. I compared Cambrell with Horace Cudbird.

Cudbird, while waiting his turn at the targets, was listening to Lucy Chigwidden talking expressively about chapterisation. Or it may have been about the interior monologue. The point is that Cudbird, an uncultivated person, was listening to Lucy's shop, and that Lucy despite considerable intellectual naïveté was sufficiently a woman of the world not to direct that shop wholly ineptly. That Cudbird's Beers are Best was doubtless the cardinal proposition of the brewer's existence; nevertheless he was prepared to interest himself in other propositions not remotely connected with this one. Whereas in the general conversation of Cambrell, despite its county tone, one suspected the designing volubility of the draper who hopes that one will take out one's change in ribbons. And perhaps the contrast between the two men went a little further than this. Cudbird had not Cambrell's directness of manner. He was, in an inoffensive way, almost shifty—having the wariness, certainly, of the man who has had to discover everything for himself. But the mind behind seemed to me peculiarly simple and direct.

"I wondered," said Cambrell easily, "if I might come early and join in?" He held up what was evidently a case of pistols. "I heard the popping and couldn't resist knocking off and coming over for another try."

Basil looked at his watch. It was not the most courteous way to greet an early guest and—because Basil was decidedly not gauche—it set me thinking. From Cambrell's words it was plain that he had been at the range before. It was equally plain that to-day he had been asked only to luncheon and a business talk. I felt that I could almost see those ribbons protruding from his pockets.

As if answering Basil's gesture, Cambrell glanced at his wrist-watch. "Just going twelve," he said. "I am afraid that in a few seconds you will have to stop your ears to our dreadful siren. But, unlike Cudbird's dazzling bottle, it doesn't go on for hours at a time. Good morning, Mrs. Chigwidden. Morning to you, Cudbird."

To this last salutation there was appended a sort of ghostly "my good man" which made us all slightly uncomfortable. Cecil, though still doubtless yielding to nobody in his admiration for Cambrell's sort, presented his cigarette case to Cudbird—emphatically in the matter-of-fact way in which one would perform this gesture to a neighbour in a club. The brewer shook his head with a faint grin which showed him amusedly rather than gratefully aware of the symbolism involved. "Well, well, Cambrell," he said, "if it isn't a right surprise to see you neglecting the needs of the consumer like this." His accent had broadened. He glanced at the case of pistols. "I expect it's a pretty long shot you're thinking of this morning?" He looked at us slyly and before we could quite take this in went on: "And how's the grand canteen? Not too heavy a charge on the benevolence of the firm?" He turned to Basil. "There's nothing like a really old-established firm, Sir Basil, for benevolent dealing. Some of them employ lads called industrial psychologists just to think out new schemes of benevolence all the time. But I believe Cambrell thought out the canteen himself." He shook his head in transparently simulated envy. "That's education, that is. I wouldn't be surprised if Plato or Cicero or such a one said that education is the mother of benevolence."

It struck me that a career such as Cudbird's is a training in belligerence, and that he enjoyed countering Cambrell's faintly insolent attitude with an abundance of obscure repartee. And whatever the last stroke had signified Cambrell plainly did not relish it. He turned away to Basil. "How have you been getting on, Roper, at fifty paces?"

Geoffrey and Anne, however, wanted a little more fun. "A canteen?" said Geoffrey. "You run a canteen, sir?" He planted the question as it were respectfully but firmly before Cambrell's nose.

"But surely what I think they call," said Anne, "a

dry canteen—one following the precepts of Our Ford?"

Cambrell laughed a shade uncertainly at this shame-lessly stolen witticism. "A dry canteen, certainly," he said. "If one tried to start a pub in a factory, you know, Bumbledom would have a fit—from the local licencing board right up to Whitehall. So it's just a dry canteen, with a diet scientifically worked out and so on. Ought to be an excellent thing for the operatives' health."

"The Cambrell canteen," said Geoffrey, "deserves suc-cess. But is it successful?"

Cambrell frowned and his easy manner became slightly pompous. "There is prejudice," he replied; "there is prej-udice as there always is. The idea will win its way, but at the moment we have had rather to reduce the scale of the thing."

Looking up from replenishing the magazine of a re-volver, Cudbird chuckled. "The heyday of benevolence," he said, "was in the time of the despots. 'The Benevolent Despots': I remember that in my history book at Burton Road School." He raised the weapon in his hand. "You can't be out-and-out benevolent unless you have the other fellow where you want him. Cambrell's done pretty well. He bought up all the pie-shops for a mile round—and who was to stop him from that? But then there was the pensions fund. Cambrell said that to be in on that you had to exercise normal care of the health, and that you weren't doing that if you didn't eat in the canteen." Cudbird chuckled again—rather viciously, I thought, this time. "It didn't work. It was what's called going too far. In fact, making your hands eat your own sausage and mash is truck. However scientific the cooking, it's common truck." He put a century-old bitterness into the word. "And truck's a trick the benevolent lost control of a long bit back. Cambrell must try again."

All this was uncomfortable. It was also bizarre. The setting made it bizarre. About us winter sunshine threw upon the frosted ground the shadow of the Priory ruins —threw shadows as irregular and as subtly, slowly changing as high clouds on a still day. On our left, running the full length of the range, was a long wall with blind arcading which rose to the broken windows of the lay dorter. Before us, and beyond the earth mound against which our targets stood, was the high blank wall of a gate-house—the only part of the ancient buildings which was almost intact, and one which obviated any danger should bullets fly high. To our right was the open park, with beyond its high boundary a confusion of slated roofs and the clang and crackle of electric trams. It was just after noon and the Priory stood in its own narrowed pool of shadow; as the sun sank the slow drift of this would be stalked by other shadows from without. The skeleton of Cudbird's bottle would mingle with the lengthening tower; the great smoke stack of the mills would sweep like a thwarted probing finger just short of the furthest crumbled buttress of the west wall. Meanwhile we stood with the discordant centuries thus hovering about us, a little knot of people watching a clash between the representatives of those great concerns which, fronting each other here across the narrowing triangle of the park, seemed perpetually to threaten the very existence of Belrive. Cambrell's dry canteen, Cudbird's cascading bottle, the ruins in their tranquillity and the park in its winter shroud: for a moment all these seemed to me to be suspended in some dramatic relationship. Then the significance evaporated, the tension dissolved. A revolver popped. A whiff of acrid smoke blew across the range. The shooting match was on again.

Wilfred Foxcroft had produced a magnifying glass and secured a handful of spent bullets; sitting with Lucy Chigwidden on a stone coffin and in a corner faintly warmed by the December sun, he was endeavouring to persuade her that he could group the bullets according to the weapons from which they had been fired. Geoffrey and Anne had drifted off; their voices, raised in excitement as if they were about some foolery of their own, could be heard occasionally from the direction of the house. To the right of the range, in the open park, Sir Mervyn Wale and Horace Cudbird were pacing to and fro in what appeared to be mutually satisfactory casual talk. Hubert Roper and Cecil Foxcroft were also isolated together: Hubert facing his nephew and gesticulating persuasively; Cecil looking, as I thought, somewhat pettishly displeased: it might be guessed that the proposed portrait was being discussed. I was myself turning back towards the range after an uneasily meditative stroll. Basil and Cambrell were in front of me, competing together in alternate shots at rather short range. I noticed that for perhaps a minute they had been silent: Basil absorbed in the targets; Cambrell puffing at a pipe. Just as I drew near they had a brief conversation. Of this and its immediate sequel I was, I believe, the only observer. Cambrell's rather baffling trick was the subject of general speculation afterwards. Basil and I alone saw the thing happen.

They had been practising taking aim, shutting their eyes and firing after a count of five or ten—a searching test, apparently, of a steady arm. It was Cambrell's turn. He stood looking fixedly at the target, his hands by his sides. Suddenly he turned right-about with military precision, so that the range was directly behind him. His right arm went up and across his chest; his revolver disappeared under his left armpit. There was a report; I heard Basil exclaim; I saw Cambrell still staring straight before him, a faint curl of smoke from the revolver mingling with the faint curl of smoke from the pipe in his left hand. Basil strode towards the target and I somehow expected him—Cecil's habit, I suppose, was in my mind—to exclaim: "Oh, good shot!"

Basil said: "A gunman's trick. I think I could do it myself."

CHAPTER VII

OF LUNCHEON that day what sticks in my mind is Cecil Foxcroft eating roast duck.

There is, I suppose, no reason why roast duck should not appear on a luncheon table, particularly in chilly weather a few days before Christmas. There was clearly no reason why, when this dish was offered, Cecil should not address himself to it. But while doing so he might have kept off the theme of Sabine fare.

Cecil was sitting next to Horace Cudbird. And Cudbird, I saw, was a novelist *in posse*. What was in a man he had an instinct to extract and weigh. From Lucy Chigwidden he had extracted the interior monologue and I don't doubt that he had been able to estimate accurately enough the degree of penetration which Lucy brought to the subject. From Cecil he was extracting a number of propositions on public schols. Moulding character, the team spirit, trusting the boys, the healthy mind in the healthy body: these hoary counters—to Cudbird perhaps as unfamiliar as Lucy's equally well-worn dicta on the craft of fiction—were disgorged by Cecil with all the appearance of being the fruits of his own laborious thought. It was charitable to feel that he grossly overdid it; that he was without artistic sense. But I wondered if this was indeed the explanation, or if it was simply that Cecil had grown like that. I have sometimes suspected that the classically trained mind is for some

reason peculiarly prone to just such an appalling atrophy.
And as I rejected the duck I found myself wondering
whether Cudbird was not engaged in formulating to
himself very much the same suspicion. The feeling was
growing on me—perhaps on a good many of us—that
Cudbird was a very clever man.

Sabine fare. Cecil was for giving boys this in abundance. An abundantly spare diet, the argument seemed
to run. Cecil paused to sum it up. He slightly frowned,
clearly striving to quarry from the virgin rock of speech
the finally pregnant phrase. He succeeded. "Plain living
and high thinking, Mr. Cudbird," he said, "is what expresses the ideal best."

My attention wandered. When it returned Cecil was
addressing himself to the delicate theme of the Emotional Life. "At the beginning of the spring term," he
was saying; "—for it seems *particularly* necessary then—
I give them a little talk on what I call Control." He
paused. "And we stop sausages or anything of that sort
for breakfast."

Anne Grainger, sitting on the other side of Cecil, was
not at all disposed to let this opportunity for outrageous
commentary pass. "Don't Cecil and his house-masters,"
she asked the table in her clear voice, "just sit pretty?
Every pound of sausages knocked off the butcher's order
is one more stroke in the cause of virginity."

I was malicious enough to feel that Cecil had asked
for it; I was old enough to feel that young women should
not talk in quite that way. What Cudbird thought I
don't know; he looked uncomfortable for the first time
within my observation. But Anne was pleased with the

little silence she had produced. She turned to Wale. "Don't you think so, Sir Mervyn? Don't you think that Cecil has a mastery of physiological fact?"

"I think that in pedagogy," said Wale, "there is much bad thinking about ends, and much worse information about means."

The unkindness of this was scarcely concealed by its being framed as a general proposition, and the words in themselves would have been enough to set me meditating anew on the problematical relationship between Cecil and Wale. But the words, spoken with the level severity of cultivated argument, had been winged with something quite other. Hate is almost the rarest of the passions to appear on the surface of civilised life. Scorn, indignation, disgust, anger, malice—all common enough—are none of them the same thing. I was at a loss for any reason why Wale should let, of all things, simple hate slip into his comment on his apparent crony Cecil. Hate it had been —and I found myself glancing at Lucy. It was so much her pigeon; so like one of those sudden eruptions of improbable uncharitableness in which characters who are all presently to be suspected of homicide are prone to indulge. But Lucy, characteristically, was not listening; she sat in an abstraction hearkening to ditties of no tone; to voices speaking within her that were not the voices of human kind. I turned back to my problem. Had Wale and Cecil quarrelled over a mistress, a sum of money— or any of the prizes for which men fight? It seemed excessively improbable. And I remembered a poem of Yeats in which it is remarked with penetration that an intellectual hatred is the worst. Likely enough Cecil's woolly, moralistic and rag-bag mind offended Wale's scientific temper. Likely enough it was that. But it remained puzzling all the same.

I turned to Cecil. Civilised man, I reflected, retains dangerously little of the sense of danger. But perhaps it was a matter of ear. I should have been scared if just that quality of voice had come in my direction. Cecil, no doubt, had simply not heard. Indeed he seemed to have been deaf not only to the implicit emotion but to the mere prose statement; he showed no resentment at having been charged with a muddled mind on his own field. Anything so outrageous simply failed to find the passages to his mind. On ordered freedom, on preparation for the battle of life, on the sense of fair play he continued to discourse throughout luncheon. And I noticed that Wale, as if with the instinct of a man who fears to have betrayed himself, took occasion to interpolate a number of civil and colourless observations.

The meal ended; it was the last placid meal that Belrive was to enjoy. Basil led Ralph Cambrell away to his study, presumably for that business talk for which he had come to the Priory. At the door my cousin turned round to us with an apology. "Will you all amuse yourselves? And, Lucy, will you look after tea again? I have a lot to do—there's an appeal I must get out—and I shall probably be working right through to dinner. Cudbird, can you possibly stop for that?"

Cudbird replied that he could not stop, but would return. And on that Basil and Cambrell disappeared and the rest of us went our several ways. I took myself off to the library, where I was presently joined by Lucy, once more draped in proofs. Feeling some reason to apprehend the emergence of the interior monologue, together with a good deal of reluctance to confront it at this slightly somnolent hour, I took down a heavy extra-illustrated history of Belrive—my favourite among Basil's treasures—and applied myself to it at a lectern. For some time Lucy's pencil strayed about her galleys and I read in silence.

"Arthur," said Lucy suddenly, "I have a suspicion."

I believe I started slightly; certain curious speculations of my own may already have been forming themselves deep in my mind. "A suspicion?" I replied. "Believe me, you must have a whole cornucopia of them. They represent your way of life."

"I have," said Lucy firmly, "*a suspicion.*"

"You mean"—I turned away reluctantly from my folio —"about Basil's appeal?"

"Basil's appeal?" Lucy rummaged for her pencil and finally found it in its commercial position behind her ear. "What is Basil's appeal?"

We were completely at cross-purposes. "You have a suspicion," I countered, "about what?"

"About this evening's mystery, of course. Basil's Mr. X."

I had forgotten about Basil's Mr. X, the unknown who was coming to dinner and who was to be a special treat for one of us. "What you suspect," I said, "is that Mr. X is going to be a special treat for you."

Lucy lost her pencil again. "However did you guess that?" she asked.

This was awkward. It was evident that Lucy was the only person among us for whom it would occur to one to prepare a surprise of this sort—like something beguilingly wrapped up in coloured paper on a children's Christmas tree. While I was casting about for some vague reply Lucy went off at a tangent. "Arthur," she said, "I have been thinking about *The Golden Bowl*."

If Lucy had announced that she had been thinking about *The Hound of the Baskervilles* or *The Woman in White* I might have stayed. As it was, I got up hastily and looked at my watch. "Half-past two," I said. "And I promised to look in on this studio affair of Hubert's."

Lucy rose too, scattering her proofs about the floor. "But how interesting. I think I'll come with you."

This again was awkward. That I had made any such promise was a lie, invented on the spur of the moment to save me from a discussion of the higher fiction. I had even no reason to suppose that Hubert would at all welcome an investigation of his activities. But I was fairly caught. Lucy retrieved her pen from the recesses of a large chair, put her bag where she was sure to remember it behind the clock, brilliantly cached her papers in the coal-scuttle and preceded me from the room.

We found the painters, father and son, in a large attic on the north side of the house—and with them Cecil, uneasily islanded amid much inexplicable professional activity. Geoffrey Roper was on top of a step-ladder, tacking a large sheet of some gauze-like material across a skylight. Hubert was abstractedly setting up a surprisingly large canvas on an easel; every now and then he would break off from this and wander off to a table which was already littered with sketches. He would study these for a time and then look sombrely at Cecil; to the entrance of Lucy and myself he gave not the slightest attention.

"Of course," Hubert was saying, "Cecil is not uninteresting in himself." He accorded his nephew a perfunctory smile which was meant, I supposed, to be the essence of tact.

"Oh, quite." Geoffrey on his perch spoke in the tones of a man who inwardly does not at all agree. "I say nothing against Cousin Cecil. There is some good bony structure here and there. Still, it's not a commission, is it? It seems a chance."

Cecil, I inferred, being a relation and not a fashionable client, could be dealt with in a spirit of light-hearted—or perhaps of absorbed—experiment. And this supposition was presently confirmed by a succession of bumping noises outside and the entrance of Basil's butler, chauffeur and gardener's boy staggering under the weight of a vast gilt-framed mirror. This was placed against the wall under Hubert's direction and the men went away. Some minutes later the butler and chauffeur returned carrying between them a cheval-glass; behind them came a house-maid with one of those circular, concave mirrors which are still a common adornment of drawing-rooms.

Hubert looked about the bare attic. "Later I shall have to work in some sort of *décor*. A bedroom, I think—lavish, overfurnished, feminine."

"A big bed," said Geoffrey, "with grey tones in the coverlet. And a single mule—"

"A mule?" interrupted Cecil—envisaging himself, I

think, as depicted in bed with some monstrous pet.

Geoffrey nodded. "A sort of woman's slipper, that is. And viridian, I should say, to tone up the whole composition."

"All the movement," said Hubert, "might start from the mule."

"What about Cecil *holding* the mule?" demanded Geoffrey, as if suddenly inspired. "The viridian mule and his rather pasty hand: now just what would one get from that? Some rather interesting values, I should say."

Cecil shifted uneasily on the single hard chair with which the attic was provided. "Really," he said, "I hardly think it appropriate to represent an unmarried man—"

"But at the moment"—Hubert was quite unheeding— "the interesting thing is the edges. In the big glass there will be the reflection of Cecil reflected in the cheval-glass. One should get some odd edges out of that."

Geoffrey shook his head. "I think, Dad, it should be the other way round. Use the big glass as a powerful diagonal. . . ."

Suddenly father and son were arguing fiercely. The servants, still standing about to shift the mirrors, stared; Cecil continued to wriggle; Lucy and I endeavoured to follow with the air of artists in a line of our own. And presently Hubert was flourishing his sketches in Geoffrey's face. "You opinionated young puppy," he cried, "do you realise that I've been hard at work on this sort of thing for months—slaving at it till I've felt like Alice and the looking-glass? And then you come walking in from your flat geometrical pap and lay down the law! Get out of it!" He turned round with a sweeping gesture. "And the rest of you too. You make the whole room a mess."

We went—Lucy, Geoffrey and myself down one stair-case and the servants down another. There is nothing sinister in what is called an exhibition of artistic tempera-ment, and the little performance put up by Hubert and Geoffrey was, if anything, mildly exhilarating. This could not be said of the quarrel into which we descended in the hall. Quarrel is perhaps the wrong word, for there was only one active participant. The thing might be called the Cambrell incident. Subsequently, it offered a good deal of matter for speculation. At the time, it was embarrassing merely.

A voice said: "Forty, perhaps?" The tones suggested leisured debate; they rose, however, above the sound of footsteps briskly crossing an uncarpeted floor. "Forty-five." The voice was louder—partly because it was ad-vancing through the inner hall at the end of which stood Basil's study; partly because urgency was creeping into its smoothness.

A second voice offered a monosyllabic reply; the foot-steps continued. Ralph Cambrell, it dawned on me, was making Basil some sort of proposition. And Basil was showing him out.

As we came down the last flight they appeared. Basil made with deliberation for the outer lobby; Cambrell turned aside to pick up a coat and hat. The coat he began to put on; then he stopped and strolled across the hall to study a picture. "I've always admired your Guardi," he said casually. "It isn't for sale?"

"Yes," said Basil matter-of-factly, "it is."

"Fifteen hundred?"

"Yes. Will you take it under your arm?"

Cambrell laughed dubiously. "I'll send round, and I count myself thoroughly lucky—really grateful. Now surely forty-five is more than—"

Basil had got hold of Cambrell's hat. He handed it to him. And because it was Basil the action was not rude; it was politely ruthless. "I prefer the other idea," he said. "And there's an end on't."

His guest made that motion with his eyebrows which is the Saxon equivalent of shrugged shoulders and gesturing hands. "My dear Roper, of course you must decide as you choose. And I wish you all good luck."

Nothing could have been more proper than this pretty speech; it relieved us of some of the discomfort we felt at stumbling upon what was none of our business as we scuttled hastily across the hall. And nothing more, I believe, would have happened but for the accident with the hat.

Cambrell dropped it—a clumsiness betraying suppressed emotion. He bent to pick it up, and as he straightened himself his face flushed dark red. "You damned fool," he cried, "even your idiot paint-splashing brother would have more sense!"

He was gone. Basil strolled over to the Guardi, glanced at it, and turned to me as I was disappearing into the library. "Do you think, Arthur, that Cambrell really cares for the arts?" And as I made some inarticulate reply he took a notebook from his pocket. "Fifteen hundred," he said, "—and you are a witness." He smiled faintly and jotted with a pencil. "Every little helps."

CHAPTER VIII

TEA, though not this time marked by the horror of intellectual games, was restless. It came into a library about which people were uneasily prowling and had no sedative effect. We balanced cups on inadequate ledges amid cliffs of books; wandering round the long dusky room we laid snail-like trails of crumbs across the floor.

Cecil was the centre of disturbance. I imagine that the roast duck had made him disinclined for further recruitment till dinner and that the sight of the Belrive muffins irked him. He had mislaid Law's *Serious Call to a Devout and Holy Life:* this ethical inconvenience he was allowing nobody to forget. Lucy too was on the hunt—first for her proofs in the coal-scuttle, next for her bag behind the clock, and finally for a great deal of note paper. With this last she proceeded to construct a dummy book of the blank-paged sort which publishers mysteriously find it expedient to create before they begin to set up type. Lucy's idea was to mark in the chapter-heads and so, by turning over the pages, to get the physical feel of the chapters: the physical feel being a new aspect of her problem which had just occurred to her. We all helped to fold the pages into some semblance of the gatherings of a book; assembly was nearly complete when Lucy let the whole thing slip and the floor was littered with the debris of her project. This produced a mixture of polite scramble and acid comment—Wale leading the scramble, Anne the comment, and Wilfred being vigorously active on both fronts.

"Has *nobody*," asked Cecil accusingly when this diversion was over, "seen my *Serious Call?*"

"Talking of serious calls," said Wilfred, "I must write to a fellow about his margins." He began to prowl about peering into ink pots.

"In his picture," said Geoffrey, "Cousin Cecil shall have the mule in one hand and Law's *Serious Call* in the other. Behind him the concave mirror shall reflect a distorted version of Titian's *Sacred and Profane Love*. It will be a problem picture in the hoary old manner and quite the success of the year." He nodded at his father. "Veteran painter's perplexing vision."

Anne put down her cup. "Sir Mervyn should have his place in the composition. Whither Cecil goes—"

I saw Wale looking more than startled at this impossible personality and judged it well to intervene hastily. "I have always felt," I said, "that tea is the turning point of the day."

The remark was meant to be soothing rather than meaningful. But Anne considered it gravely. "A sentiment," she asked with deliberation, "which marks Uncle Arthur as of the turned rather than the turners?"

"The day," said Geoffrey, "carries him on its great arc from morn to evening. And, supine, he murmurs such aphorisms as these."

The gibberish of these young people was becoming wholly tiresome. I was about to brace my mind to the not-too-stretching task of evolving some more cogent witticism in reply when Anne took up her part in the verbal pit-pat again. "But what," she asked, "will Uncle Arthur do when Hesperus nightly cries banishment from the bed of his bride Belrive?"

"The sword," said Geoffrey, "thrust between the sheets at ten P. M. sharp."

"Hurry up, Uncle Arthur, it's time. Hurry up, please, it's time."

Cecil, who had been poking after William Law's masterpiece in a dark corner, turned round abruptly. "What extravagant nonsense are you talking, Anne?"

"Haven't you gathered? Cousin Basil is selling Belrive to Horace Cudbird to build the world's biggest pub."

"On the contrary"—Geoffrey shook his head—"he is selling the place to Ralph Cambrell to run more Cambrell benevolence. Cambrell houses, shops and cinema. The week will begin with worship in a Cambrell chapel and end with football and hockey on Cambrell fields under the Cambrell code. A happy self-contained community financed by Cambrell all round. For the study of the ruins a Cambrell Archæological Society will be formed."

Cecil sat down abruptly. "Why ever should Basil do either of these abominable things?"

"To reach the moon," said Anne. "Again, haven't you heard? There is to be a great rocket winging through space. And Geoffrey and I are putting in for the job of pilots. Like the interstellar necking party in Wells' film. We look at the moon and feel there may be a square deal in those argent fields."

"Actually," said Geoffrey, "the idea is to start a meteorological station in the antarctic. A great deal of money is required: that's what Basil's appealing for. As human purposes go it has much to commend it."

"But surely"—Cecil was looking round him in bewilderment—"Basil cannot legally—"

His brother Wilfred gave a muffiny snort. "I don't believe a word of it. But if it were true I know who could stop him."

"Lucy, might I after all have a cup of tea?"

The voice at the door was Basil's; the effect upon the company in the library was discomposing in the extreme.

"If you will allow me to carry it off, that is."

"The *Serious Call*," said Cecil loudly. "I wonder if any of you has seen my *Serious Call*?"

Wilfred put down his muffin. "That fellow's margins," he said. "Really must get off a note." He peered into the nearest ink pot.

I changed early that evening and was back in the library by seven o'clock. It would be half an hour before the dressing bell rang. But there was nobody about, and I concluded that most people had gone to their rooms early. When one has been only too much a member of a family a little solitude is a natural resource. And a large house can thus mysteriously untenant itself. In Lucy's stories there is always some animation. The door—of kitchen, billiard-room, boudoir, pantry—is opened, and there on the other side is invariably somebody ready and eager to keep things going. Actually, such wanderings are likely to be lonely as a cloud. And this is particularly so with family parties, during which only servants are aware of how much time people put in skulking in their own fastnesses.

These are relevant reflections. Later that night I had stoutly to maintain against a good deal of covert incredulity that between seven o'clock and ten to eight I encountered no living soul at Belrive.

Of course I went out. And that I went out was to seem highly suspicious. We are all sentimental—and yet how unaccountable a dash of sentiment in one's actions may make them appear!

I like the place in the dark. And—it is a sad admission —I particularly like the ruins in the phantasmagoric light of Cudbird's bottle. Half-close one's eyes in a fire-lit room and one can see what shapes one wills stirring in the corners and flitting across the ceiling; wander among the ruins in that fluctuating twilight of commercial enterprise and one can see cloister and dorter, night stair and warming-room possessed once more by those who first laid stone on stone in the building of this ancient place. What daylight shows as a crumbled chapel and a ruined choir one can dream of as a great design well begun.

At about ten past seven I opened the front door and stepped out on the terrace. It was icy cold: earlier in the day it had been chilly enough but now the temperature had suddenly dropped and I knew that we were in for a black frost. I hesitated and, stepping indoors again, secured a heavy coat which I had left in a cloakroom by the outer lobby. I found too my galoshes—the possession of such things dates me sadly, I fear—and slipped them over my pumps. I crossed the terrace and leant for a moment on its high balustrade. It will be as well to confess at once that I was in considerable agitation of mind.

Crossing the hall I had glanced at the square little Guardi which Basil had so briskly sold to Ralph Cambrell. For the painter I do not greatly care—he is a mannerist to my mind—but the impending disappearance even of this restless and inconsiderable heirloom startled me. The deal might have been over a red setter or a second-hand car.

And Basil was fond of that school; I remembered that he had once bought a Canaletto. Whatever his project was, he was in earnest. If Belrive was his to dispose of, it would go. And that Basil did not know exactly what he could, and could not, do seemed to me very unlikely indeed. I stared into the dark and tried to grasp the thing. He was just the man. And there was nothing vulgar or unbeseeming in the scheme. It had its own worth. Indeed, if one were to cast about in the modern world for something roughly analogous to the monastic idea the project of secluding oneself in a frozen solitude in quest of knowledge might be as near an equivalent as one would find. All this I realised.

I turned in my mind from Basil to his brother Hubert, the legitimate heir of everything around me. He had certainly been told: that was what he had meant in speaking of Basil's formal dealing and expedition. How must he feel? Reviewing the day which had passed I concluded that he did feel something; his sombre mood linked itself to what was going forward. Instinct told me that not even to tap the energy of the atom nor yet to paint like Giorgione or Cézanne would Hubert Roper sell an acre his fathers gave him. But were his brother to do so would he protest? Would he passionately re-

sent the thing? Would he accept it absolutely? Or
would his reaction be somewhere in between? I made
the chastening discovery that to the solution of this
enigma not all my professional sense of character enabled
me to hazard a guess. About painters—far more than
about musicians—there is an absolute inarticulateness;
they can communicate in pigment alone; this, maybe,
serves to make them more baffling than most.

Again the cold caught me. I stamped my feet on the
flags and then went briskly down a flight of steps to
the garden. Indeterminate light—from the distant bottle,
from lamps in the drive, from a fugitive sickle moon—
lay on a frozen lily pond; I tested the ice and judged
it near to bearing. The noise of the traffic, usually a confused hubbub, came out of the night in a symphony of
distinguishable sounds: the flat patter of wood or leather
on concrete; the crack of some skin of ice beneath a
tyre; far away, and faint as its evocations were massive,
a brass band playing *Hark, the Herald Angels Sing*. A
tram clanging and clattering by drowned the music; a
succession of sparks, crackling amid the wires as it took
a corner, lit up the terrace as with a faint lightning and
I thought I discerned by this unexpected illumination
the figure of a man leaning with his back against the
balustrade. A motive of curiosity made me linger on the
chance of another shower of sparks revealing more. Another tram passed, but without producing any fortuitous
flashlight. I lit a cigarette and leaning against a stone
seat glanced upwards at the house: on the bedroom floor
nearly every window showed some glimmer of light.

A few minutes later I turned away and entered the park. The brass band had come nearer; plangent now, it was scarcely drowned even by the sudden explosive uproar of a motor bicycle starting up near the gates. I had intended merely a reflective stroll of fifteen minutes. But I had much to occupy me—I was still revolving the fate of Belrive—and it was just short of ten to eight when I arrived at the front door. A light was burning in the porch. Under it stood a young man in a dark overcoat and evening clothes. He had just stepped back from ringing the bell.

I believe I was disconcerted. There is always something slightly awkward in such a convergence upon a fellow guest who is unknown to one. In town it is very common for people who have presumably enjoyed the advantages of breeding simply to ignore anyone so encountered—much as one might do if one arrived together with the linkmen and the hairdresser and the caterers. But if I was disconcerted it was not merely by a momentary impulse in myself to this depraved conduct. I remembered that this must be Mr. X.

Basil, it struck me, ought to have dissipated the mystery before his guest arrived. It was not quite courteous to the young man, who doubtless thought of himself as Mr. Smith or Mr. Brown, to have him present himself on the doorstep in the character of an enigma. . . .

By the time that I had got through these unnecessary reflections the young man had wished me good evening. I responded, and as I did so the door opened. A familiar parlourmaid, the familiar lobby, the hall with its great fire beyond—so much I had time to take in. And then the thing happened—happened with the smooth rapidity of good melodrama. A female voice cried out in terror or alarm and a moment later a second maidservant ran into the hall. The young man beside me—who had as I suppose been about to murmur his host's name—took a swift step forward and checked himself; and even as he did so the breathless girl in the hall found voice. "Help," she cried, "help! Sir Basil is killed!"

It was like a cue. There was the sound of a door thrown open and a man's figure appeared silhouetted against the fire. It was Basil himself. "Jane," he said with mild severity, "what is the meaning of this?"

Jane behaved in the conventional way of one who sees a ghost. She screamed, swayed, collapsed. And hard upon this appeared Richards, Basil's butler. He spoke without agitation. "It's Mr. Wilfred, Sir Basil. He appears to have been shot—badly wounded. Shall I—"

I had been listening horror-struck and dumbfounded. Now I believe I cried out and almost collapsed myself. The young man, who was still standing beside me, took me by the arm. "A relation of yours?" he asked quietly.

We were moving into the hall. I shook my head. "A distant kinsman only. But . . ."

Richards was at the telephone. Basil, hurrying across the hall pale and stern, skirted the recumbent body of Jane. The parlourmaid who had answered the door was emitting tentative sobs. And hurrying down the stairs with dangling braces came Sir Mervyn Wale, looking very upset indeed.

All this the young man observed. Then, almost imperceptibly, he sighed.

"When one dines out," he murmured, "one scarcely expects to be served with one's own pigeon as promptly as this."

CHAPTER IX

WE NEVER discovered how Basil had come to make the acquaintance of John Appleby, nor how Appleby came to be in our part of the world. We had to content ourselves with the fact that within what appeared to be minutes of the shooting of Wilfred Foxcroft a young detective-inspector from Scotland Yard had rung the bell and proceeded to look circumspectly about him. The effect ought to have been reassuring—like that of the unobtrusive person who rises from a corner of the railway-carriage and says "I am a doctor" when somebody has fallen down in a faint. Actually the revelation of Appleby's way of life was unnerving in an extreme.

Not that he appeared to push himself into the incident that had befallen; he held on to his hat until it became clear that the situation was not one from which he had best withdraw with the murmured words of the untimely guest. But he was from the first professionally observant. The house party gathered in the hall member by member—hushed, clamorous, confused, controlled as the temper of each dictated. Appleby stood in a corner and gave to everyone the roving but sufficient attention of a competent critic making preliminary observations in an unfamiliar gallery. He was impassive, but once or twice his eyes grew slightly round. I found myself thinking of the pleasure of a small boy who discovers how something works.

Wale's voice came from the study. "Casualty," he was saying. "Casualty . . . Dr. Mervyn Wale . . . to Belrive Priory at once. And I want the R.S.O. . . . I said Sir Mervyn Wale . . . R.S.O. . . ."

Basil, staring into the fire, roused himself. "The police," he said. "I suppose we must have the police."

"Ashton? Never heard of him. I must have Badger." Wale's unimpassioned voice came from the telephone still. "I don't care who your senior man is. I am Mervyn Wale . . . Badger."

Wale was enjoying himself. He would get Badger. And I supposed the young man Appleby to be enjoying himself too. I wondered whom he would get.

"I suppose," said Basil, "I had better ring them up when Wale is finished." He looked interrogatively at his new guest.

"Oh, decidedly," said Appleby. He spoke with a slight nervous diffidence: I wondered if it was the professional manner of the higher branches of his calling. "Perhaps I might do it for you?"

Surprisingly, the parlourmaid who had opened the door stopped crying. "The other line, sir," she said to Basil. "It will be free."

Basil nodded and led Appleby into the lobby. Wale's voice came again. "I want to speak to Mr. Badger. If he is at dinner be so good as to tell him it is Sir Mervyn Wale."

"Detective-Inspector Appleby." The voice came from the lobby. "Is Inspector Leader still on duty there? Haines? No, I don't want Haines. Put me through to Inspector Leader's house. . . ."

"My dear Badger, how are you? Yes . . . yes . . . but my game has gone sadly to pieces, I fear. . . . I wonder, could you come to the infirmary at once? A rather ticklish thing . . ."

"Leader, I wonder could you possibly come along to Sir Basil Roper's at once? Somebody shot . . . yes, but I rather felt that Haines . . . capital. Yes, I'll take a look round."

It was all very efficient. But I found myself unreasonably resentful that we were to be deprived of the services of Ashton and Haines; I had a momentary suprarational conviction that Badger and Leader were lesser men. The end of life is action and we instinctively rebel against decisions made while we have to stand passively by. I was meditating this evidence of human imbecility —there was nothing better to do—when the front door was pushed open and Horace Cudbird came in.

"Is anyone ill?" he asked soberly. "There's an ambulance on the drive."

We dined at about a quarter to nine. Inspector Leader was in the study, making what observations he judged useful. Young Mr. Appleby, on the other hand, was sitting beside Lucy Chigwidden as had been planned—an arrangement which made us all acutely aware that the evening had produced a more shattering surprise than any Mr. X could afford. Richards, no doubt upon a nice calculation of proprieties, had left Wilfred's and Wale's places undisturbed. In the absence of the still distraught Jane he was also handing fish; this trifling variation upon the customary ritual of Basil's table struck me in my slightly dazed state as the most extraordinary circumstance of all.

News, good or bad, might come from the hospital at any time: nevertheless it had seemed reasonable to eat. This presented no difficulty; we consumed what was set before us. Our conversation, however, we had to choose, and for some time there was difficulty in deciding where to begin. It occurred to me—I fear in somewhat macabre vein—that it would have been simpler had Wilfred been killed outright. We should then have been silent, or conceivably have spoken sparingly of other things. As it was, we were left guessing both as to the gravity of what had occurred and as to its meaning. Cecil was the first person who endeavoured to take soundings.

"This," said Cecil—and he glanced round the table as if to command general attention to an important utterance—"this is a very distressing thing."

There was a distressed silence.

"A most distressing and disturbing thing."

"Cousin Cecil," said Anne, "makes wonderfully articulate the sentiment of us all." She paused. "But of course with the extra warmth which only a brother can feel."

Appleby gave my appalling niece the most fleeting glance. He seemed to find much to engage his attention on the plate before him.

"I may say"—Cecil was not at all discomposed—"that I have had my apprehensions lest something of the sort should occur. With firearms there is *always* an element of danger."

This was unchallengeable; nobody spoke.

"We have a rifle-range for the O.T.C. I impose the most stringent regulations upon the boys."

In Appleby's face I thought I could discern the satisfaction of a supposition confirmed.

"Both instructors are always present, and there are never more than five boys at a time."

Geoffrey Roper put down his glass. "Excellent," he said. "Most sound indeed. If only Cousin Wilfred were here to mark and learn."

Appleby, having finished his fish, appeared to be giving politely furtive attention to the quality of Basil's silver. Basil said "Geoffrey" in a sterner tone than I had ever heard him use. There would have been a most uncomfortable pause had Cecil not gone straight on.

"The slightest carelessness and a possibly fatal accident may occur. Wilfred has been fiddling with those revolvers constantly."

"I think," said Basil, "that nothing is to be gained by entering on suppositions. We know too little. After this meal—which must be a hasty one—we shall place ourselves at the disposal of Inspector Leader, who will make every necessary enquiry."

This was designed as final—and only Anne would have embroidered on it. "It is quite childish," she said, "to pretend that we may assume that Wilfred shot himself accidentally." She made one of her feline pauses. "Or that he shot himself at all."

"Oh, but surely we know *something*." This was Lucy; I realised with dismay that she had surrendered her discretion to what might be termed her professional angle. "For instance, *where* was he shot?"

"In my study." Basil's firm misunderstanding was wholly forbidding.

"Through the right lung." Anne deplorably raised her voice. "I heard Sir Mervyn say so on the telephone."

"*There!*" said Lucy triumphantly. "And in a dinner-jacket. If the shot were fired from close range the whole shirt-front would be blackened with powder. Would it not, Mr. Appleby?"

Appleby was absorbedly helping himself to a fragment of steak—so absorbedly that the question had to be repeated. There was irony in the thought that it was for just this sort of thing that Mr. X had been invited to Belrive. And I was mildly delighted when Mr. X offered by way of reply only an inane social smile.

The young man's position was obviously difficult. His own pigeon was indeed being served up at Belrive; but not, as it were, at the particular table to which he had been a bidden guest. At the end of dinner he could, of course, go away. I suspected, however, that this was not in his mind. I had an uneasy feeling that as a collection of human beings we had rapidly come to interest Appleby quite a lot; I even suspected that the little manœuvre over Inspectors Haines and Leader had represented a first move in some plan to insinuate himself into our perplexities. And of this some confirmation presently emerged. Richards, who had been out of the room, reappeared somewhat dubiously at the door. He moved towards Basil; then, changing his mind, he turned to Appleby. "The inspector of police, sir," he said, "would be glad if you could join him in the study."

Appleby looked at Basil. His expression—compounded

of apology, surprise, and willingness to act as his host should desire—was very nicely suited to the occasion.

There was a little silence. "Mr. Appleby," said Basil formally—I could see that the two men were the merest acquaintances—"if you can give your local colleague any help it will, of course, be a kindness to us as well as to him."

It was all rather solemn. Appleby looked decently hesitant. "Leader," he said, "is an excellent man. You can have great confidence in him, Sir Basil." He laid his table-napkin beside his plate. "But perhaps I ought to do anything I can." He rose and with sudden large strides was out of the room.

"The bloodhound unleashed." Geoffrey Roper was endeavouring to catch Richards' eye in the hope of more claret. But Richards, having very properly decided that the occasion was one on which drink should be poured at his employer's nod alone, was giving absorbed attention to a *café filtre*. "A most presentable bloodhound. For Aunt Lucy a very glass of fashion and mould of form. Quite the new sort of bloodhound. Endless uncles in the Foreign Office and belongs to at least half a dozen exclusive clubs."

Horace Cudbird, who had said nothing throughout our thoroughly constrained meal, looked up suddenly as one who will rebut a slander. "It can't be denied," he said, "that winning a county scholarship has led the lad to pick up south-country ways. But his grandfather baked the best bread in Stonegate."

"And was intimately acquainted with Jim Meech and the canaries." Anne was smiling impertinently at Cudbird. "The bloodhound, in fact, is late-risen from the *canaille*. Always more sagacious than the highly bred strains. Consider Cousin Cecil. Could he avenge Wilfred? Well, could he?"

"Would he?" said Geoffrey, and gloomily drained the dregs in his glass.

"Need he?" Geoffrey's father spoke for the first time. "Surely it is most extravagant to suppose that this is a matter of crime? Wilfred was quite as careless with those revolvers as Cecil suggests."

"Safety catches," I said, "and Verona drops."

Hubert nodded. "His zest for trivial lores. He fancies himself among other things a gunsmith."

"I don't know"—Basil pushed his coffee cup away from him—"that Wilfred has ever fancied himself as a genie or sprite."

"Though he might readily be conceived," said Geoffrey, "as a goblin."

"Or," said Anne, "as a satyr."

"I mean," continued Basil evenly, "that he might very well shoot himself, accidentally or otherwise. But he could hardly ensure that the weapon be spirited away forthwith. And certainly no weapon has been found. Lucy's point moreover, though not perhaps raised in a very timely way, was sound. About the powdermarks. Wilfred was not shot from particularly close range."

For the first time, I think, there was general recognition of what we were facing. Cecil reacted characteristically and at once. "Robbery," he declared. "There has undoubtedly been either robbery or an attempt at it." He looked genuinely alarmed. "The house must be searched."

"I think it likely," said Hubert, "that they will search more than the house."

"They will search the family history," said Geoffrey.

"They will search the wind," said Anne, "—to see what is in it."

"They will search," said Geoffrey, "the heart."

"Known enemies."

"Blackmail . . . the past."

"Beneficiaries."

"Women . . . jealousy."

"Where were *you* when the shot was fired?"

"Who last saw the . . ."

The telephone bell rang shrilly in the lobby.

CHAPTER X

ANNE GRAINGER was rather more than normally athletic; nevertheless there was something startling in the lithe speed with which she was out of the room. I wondered if Geoffrey, whose callousness was of the genuine and thoroughgoing sort artists sometimes develop, realised just how she had been waiting for that ring. For I was convinced that Anne, whatever her normal attitude to her guardian might be, had been sitting through this meal in a condition of intolerable strain. It was this that had given her talk—never wholly beautiful—its extravagant impropriety.

She came back, quite slowly, her lips parted in an expression I had never seen before. "They have removed the bullet," she said. "He is still unconscious. Wale is on his way back. They think"—she hesitated—"they think he may pull through."

Cecil offered up a pious ejaculation—loudly, as if quite determined to be heard in the right quarter. The rest of us were silent, and in the silence I found myself trying to interpret Anne's voice. All but suppressed in it there had been a tone of incredulity. Perhaps she had given up Wilfred for dead. Perhaps, on the contrary, she had until this moment shut out of her mind the mere possibility of such an issue. I tried to imagine in just what circumstances I should myself look like that, speak like that. . . . And I told myself that it might conceivably be if I found some dream or nightmare come true.

We had abandoned the dinner table; now Basil made for the door. "Those fellows in the study had better be told," he said. "And it is about time I had some conversation with them myself. Yes, Richards?"

The butler had come in as if with a message; he was an old servant of the family to whom I was considerably attached; I was surprised to notice him glancing at me with mild disapproval.

"Inspector Leader, Sir Basil, would be greatly obliged if Mr. Ferryman would come to the study."

It was awkward and odd. The request was unaccountable in itself, and it had been issued from Basil's study just as the study's owner had announced his intention of proceeding there himself. We were made abruptly aware that Belrive was no longer a self-contained, self-controlled community. It had become the business of the police to investigate our affairs. And they had their own way of setting about it.

"I suppose I had better go," I said. The remark sounded rather fatuous; I might have been a small boy putting a jaunty face upon a summons before authority.

"Leader must plainly see everyone, and arrange the interviews as he wishes," said Basil. "The rest of us had better go into the library."

"When it is Cecil's turn," asked Geoffrey, "will he give them a little talk on what he calls Control?"

On this I left the dining-room, and I confess I felt some need of control myself. I do not approve of the police. This may seem a foolish statement—and indeed I

don't doubt that if I were being robbed I should call out
for the nearest constable lustily enough. I suppose I mean
that I have no great fancy for the working out of human
law. Nemesis is more impressive. At least I have an in-
vincible repugnance towards that sort of ferreting which
Geoffrey and Anne had been suggesting when the telephone rang. Walking to the study I felt that I must be
on my guard against presenting an appearance of irrational hostility.

Leader and Appleby were both standing when I entered: Leader studying something on Basil's desk; Appleby staring at the floor with a frown which I hoped
reflected a continued sense of the delicacy of his position.

"The doctors think that Mr. Foxcroft may live," I
said.

Leader grabbed a notebook—very much as if this were
something which it would be helpful to commit to paper. Appleby, I thought, looked if anything a shade disappointed; it might be suspected that he regarded Wilfred's possible recovery, attended as it would probably
be by a simple denunciation of the criminal, as likely to
dissipate a very pretty problem. Here was another strictly
professional angle.

"Mr. Ferryman?" said Leader.

"Yes."

"Mr. Ferryman, Mr. Foxcroft is a stockbroker?"

"A banker."

Leader peered at the desk before him. "Margins," he
said; "he was writing a letter about margins. I thought
it sounded financial. But what exactly would they be?"

I shook my head, feeling that this was distinctly a tangential method of investigation. "I have very little idea."

"One covers them," said Appleby helpfully. "They are something financial and one covers them. Make a note of that, Leader. And now we might experiment with the lights."

Leader scratched his chin. "You're forgetting Mr. Ferryman here."

"Not at all." Appleby seemed to be thoroughly in charge. "Mr. Ferryman will help. Do you mind? Come over here. Don't step in the blood. Please sit down at the desk."

"You struck me earlier in the evening," I said, "as quite a diffident person."

Appleby smiled the slightly absent smile with which a dentist receives the repartee of a patient. "Facing the window, Mr. Ferryman. Yes, that's just right. Leader, the switches are by the door. Only I don't at all want to disturb those curtains. So do you mind waiting? I shan't be a moment."

He disappeared. "Your colleague," I said, "has a brisk way with him."

In Leader's eye I thought I detected a sympathetic gleam. He contented himself, however, with a nod; and then fell to his notebook. I had leisure to look about me. The room was large; looking at it with a fresh eye I reflected that it might best be described as a handsome apartment. The most noticeable piece of furniture was the great desk at which I now sat. It faced an embrasure, at present curtained, in which stood as I knew a large french window giving on the terrace: to judge from an icy wind which blew about me this window must be wide open. Behind me and to my left as I sat facing this was a low standard lamp; in the wall on my left was the fireplace with a sofa and chairs; in the opposite wall was the room's only door. The walls were lined with Basil's working books; there were a number of glass cases and sliding presses with geological specimens; a large table in a corner was littered with maps and charts.

"Mr. Ferryman is unmistakable." Appleby's voice, coming from directly in front of me, made me start. He had gone out to the terrace, entered the room by the French window, and now stood a few yards away from me concealed by the curtains—through a crack in which he must be making his observations. "And now, Leader, the lights."

Leader crossed to the door and flicked at the switches. For a moment the room was in darkness save for the dancing light of the fire. Then the single standard lamp behind my left shoulder went on.

"Mr. Ferryman," came Appleby's voice, "consider yourself to be writing a letter on margins. Is that a good light in which to do so?"

"Perfectly." The soft illumination was picking out an arc upon the desk before me.

"In a way," said Appleby—and I thought his voice sounded disappointed—"it's not at all a bad light for shooting." There was a pause. "But only in a way. It would be all right if one felt that all one had to do was to shoot."

There was a rustle and his footsteps sounded on the

terrace; Leader and I were left to a few moments' sufficient meditation; then Appleby was once more in the room.

"There's not a doubt of it," he said. "We know that Mr. Wilfred Foxcroft was shot, but we have no reason at all to believe that he was shot at."

"We have," I said, "this reason: that he was shot."

Appleby glanced at me sharply. Then he smiled. "Mr. Ferryman, I have known for years that you have an exact mind. And here it is."

Leader, who might be judged not a reading man, looked puzzled and licked his pencil.

"Thank you. But it's clear enough."

"Yes. The fact that the man was shot is evidence that he was shot at. But evidence of what strength? Fire a revolver into a crowd in the dark and the weight of such evidence would sink to a cypher. Fire through these curtains at someone sitting between that standard lamp and yourself and the fact that a certain man is shot is weak evidence that it was that particular man you wanted to shoot."

"Particularly," said Leader as if inspired, "when he is sitting at another man's desk."

"And is dressed"—I was tempted to join in this not very stretching game—"in the sort of uniform that a dinner-jacket constitutes."

That the wrong man had conceivably been shot was a conception not in the circumstances very difficult to arrive at; I was disconcerted nevertheless at the speed with which Appleby had made the point. The little practical experiment too had rattled me. It was an eerie thought that sitting there in my own light I had been presenting just the silhouette which Wilfred had presented some three hours before. I glanced at the little pool of congealing blood on the carpet at my right. The thing was becoming horribly real.

"And now," said Appleby, "about Sir Basil's habits with regard to this room. It is his study. Did he regard it as more or less private, or was it treated like the other living rooms in the house?"

"Really, that is the sort of point on which you might do well to apply to our host himself."

I thought this a neat reminder; Appleby however was not at all put off. "For example, Mr. Wilfred Foxcroft came in here and started to write a letter at Sir Basil's desk. One sees how important it is to know if that was unusual. If only Sir Basil was ever known to work here . . ."

"The point," I said, "is not wholly obscure to me." And then, because I felt this attempt at irony to have been childish, I added: "It might be called slightly unusual. And I believe I know how it may have happened. Downstairs, people usually write letters in the library. But all the note paper there was used this afternoon for another purpose. I know Foxcroft had this letter to write. And finding all the library note paper gone he might very well have wandered in here."

"I see. Sir Basil works here a lot?"

"I believe so. He was working here this afternoon. I remember his saying that he would probably be working here right through to dinner."

Leader's notebook was poised in a flash. "Let me have

the names, please, of everybody who heard him say that."

The ferreting had begun. And I realised that Leader, though less forceful than his metropolitan colleague, had the right instincts. I gave the information meekly. Basil had made this remark at luncheon and it had been heard by everybody staying in the house, by Richards, by Ralph Cambrell and by Horace Cudbird. Getting all this on paper considerably slowed down the tempo of the investigation.

"Who," said Appleby, "would wish to shoot Sir Basil Roper?" He looked at me speculatively, and I was preparing to evolve a reply when I realised that the question was a rhetorical one. "But, again, who would wish to shoot Mr. Foxcroft? For, after all, it is far from certain that the shot was fired, as we have been assuming, from behind the shelter of the curtains. The assailant may have been facing Mr. Foxcroft boldly, and very well aware of what he was about. And there is a third possibility. The shot may have been intended for neither of these people."

"You mean," I asked, "that only accident may have been involved?"

"If it was an accident," interposed Leader, "where is the gun?" He turned to Appleby. "An accident with some element of criminal carelessness," he suggested. "Somebody is scared and makes off with the gun."

Appleby showed no enthusiasm for this reconstruction. "I was merely reflecting," he said, "that Mr. Foxcroft might have been taken not for Sir Basil but for somebody else. At least, this is something which we must not exclude." He glanced rather vaguely from one to the other of us. I had a feeling that his mind was really occupied elsewhere.

"May I ask," I said, "what has prompted you to call me in first in this way? I don't at all mind, but I suspect that Sir Basil is a little puzzled."

Leader, to whom I addressed this question, appeared to think it possible that the answer might be found in his notebook. It was left to Appleby to speak.

"Simply, Mr. Ferryman, that you are the only person in this house about whom we have any information. You make a natural starting point." Young Mr. Appleby met my slight frown with an amiable and deferential smile. "I understand that you are a relation, but a distant one. You will take an objective view. And—I needn't hint—a penetrating one. An investigation of this sort is largely a matter of probing human conduct, of penetrating human character. Here you are our natural ally—and one of the most effective we could find in England, if I may be impertinent enough to say so."

I had no doubt of the sufficiency of his impertinence —nor that it was accompanied by considerable intelligence. He knew that flattery may usefully be applied to the most sophisticated, particularly if not laboriously dissimulated. As the sweet barb passes the intellect notes it for what it is; it strikes down nevertheless to that uncritical level where self-esteem is all. "If you need literary counsel," I said, "you would do better to co-opt Mrs. Chigwidden." But I felt pleased all the same.

Appleby treated my reply as a very good joke indeed, and was backed by Leader with a rather belated chuckle. "Of course," he went on, "you would wish to exercise a certain discretion in discussing people you know. On the other hand you will certainly want to help."

There was no certainty in it. I do not approve of the police. My desire was entirely that the whole horrible business should be hushed up. Nevertheless I heard myself say: "Of course I will help in any way I can."

The young man looked grateful. He had just that deference which I am accustomed to meet with from young critics at literary parties. It would not have been irrelevant had I remembered how some of these behave when they get home to their flats and portable typewriters.

"Then," said Appleby, "let us sit down and get one or two matters clear."

I sat down. I think I may be said to have relaxed; I recall going so far as to begin filling my pipe. Whatever the traditional avocation of the Applebys in Stonegate, the manners of this wandering son were good. And in these times good manners are as soothing as the three or four perfect days an English summer provides.

I sat down in an easy chair. Appleby moved towards the fireplace as if to sit down there. Leader continued to stand, his notebook supported on a hand as sufficient for the purpose as a lectern.

"A quarter to eight," said Appleby. He was still moving away from me. "That's the interesting time. Mr. Ferryman"—and he swung suddenly round—"what were you doing on the terrace then?"

CHAPTER XI

I LOOKED at Appleby and he looked at me. My impression was something that of contemplating an expensive camera. Indignation would have been the natural emotion to express at the perfidious way in which the question had been led up to; what I actually contrived must have been something very like dismay.

"Was it anything," Appleby continued blandly, "which would have precluded your hearing a pistol-shot at this window?"

I recovered myself. "If you mean was I letting off fireworks or playing the loud bassoon the answer is No."

Appleby turned to Leader. "There's an idea: fireworks. But I suppose that is over in the district?"

"Quite over. Plenty for a bit before the fifth of November and then a quick tail-off. I haven't heard any now for weeks."

"Well then, the loud bassoon."

I believe Leader wrote "loud bassoon" in his notebook; it was his instinct when at a loss.

"The bassoon," continued Appleby gravely, "is a good suggestion of Mr. Ferryman's. Something of the sort was playing as I came up the drive: perhaps a Salvation Army band. But I doubt if it is quite what we want."

"What we want," I said, "is merely the general hubbub of traffic round the Priory. Motor bicycles on the hill, for instance, produce the filthiest racket. A revolver-

97

shot would pass unregarded simply because the ear is so accustomed to that."

Appleby nodded triumphantly, as if I had thought of something very bright indeed. "That's it!" he said.

"And then there is the additional fact that revolvers have been popping away all around us. Sir Basil has a range at which we have all been practising."

Leader looked as if he were going to enquire about revolver licences. Appleby glanced up sharply. "All of you? Including the two guests at luncheon—Cudbird and Cambrell?"

"Yes."

"You have yourself watched everybody having a turn?"

"Yes. It seemed the civil thing. I'm not attracted myself."

"Firearms," said Appleby as if dictating to Leader's notebook, "do not attract Mr. Ferryman. But they attract Mr. Foxcroft?"

"Yes."

"You watched quite carefully? You could provide a fairly reliable estimate of each person's degree of skill?"

I was puzzled. "Yes, I believe I could. One or two things struck me. Geoffrey Roper, who has all the delicate muscular correlations necessary to a painter, is quite surprisingly bad."

"That is very interesting." Appleby was looking absent again. "By the way, just what *were* you doing on the terrace?"

"I had been taking an evening stroll in the park."

"I see. I thought that when we met under the porch

you were slightly disturbed. I have wondered if you had happened to hear or notice anything giving cause for uneasiness."

This sort of technique was doubtless going to be applied to everyone in the house. It was clear that this time the camera must be faced squarely. "No," I said. "Nothing of the sort. When one is stopping in a house there is always a slight awkwardness in meeting a new guest on the doorstep."

"Would you mind," interposed Leader, "saying that again?" I realised with something of a shock that he was scribbling away in efficient shorthand. I repeated what I had said. It sounded extraordinarily foolish.

But Appleby agreed. He agreed and at the same time contrived to suggest respectful surprise that this embarrassment should be experienced by a man of the world so finished as myself. "These questions," he said, "must be asked of everybody"—the words came as smoothly as they come in Lucy's fictions—"as a matter of routine. We must endeavour to fix the whereabouts of everybody concerned round about a quarter to eight. At half-past seven Sir Basil was undoubtedly in this room and sitting at that desk. The parlourmaid Jane saw him there. That is why she was convinced that it was he who had been shot when she returned here at about ten to eight and saw Mr. Foxcroft's body. You remember what happened then, Mr. Ferryman. We were at the front door. Jane ran into the hall crying that Sir Basil had been killed. Sir Basil appeared and so, almost at the same moment, did Richards. Richards announced that it was Mr. Foxcroft to whom an accident had happened. I am afraid"—

Appleby glanced at me mildly—"that you were very much upset."

I felt an uncomfortable sensation in my spine. The man had the skill of a competent barrister. There was the suggestion that Wilfred had been shot in mistake for Basil; there was the suggestion that it was Richards' correction of Jane that had upset me; there was the fact that I had been wandering about outside. I had an impulse to say something about demanding the presence of a solicitor. Repressing this extravagance, I simply replied: "I was naturally much shocked."

"A shocking affair," said Leader suddenly and very solemnly. I wondered if he was recalling some official manual of etiquette.

Appleby, without expressing verbal agreement, spared a moment to looking adequately serious. "Will you give us," he asked—and I realised how firmly he had dug himself into the investigation—"a fairly detailed account of your movements this evening?"

"I changed early and came down to the library. It was just seven. There was nobody about. I glanced at a book for about ten minutes and then went to the front door and out to the terrace. It was cold; I returned to the lobby, got a coat and galoshes and once more went out to the terrace. I stood there for a few minutes, watching the big sign on the brewery. Then I went down a flight of steps—those not far from this window—and paused by a small sheet of water below. I remarked that it was frozen hard. Then I strolled off into the park and did not return until just before our meeting under the porch."

"Thank you. I suppose you met nobody during your walk?"

"No. It would be a most unlikely thing to happen."

"Quite so. And that means you saw nobody from the moment you came downstairs to the moment we met before the front door?"

I suppose I must have hesitated; at least I was aware of both Appleby and Leader looking at me very enquiringly indeed. "I did think," I said, "that I caught a glimpse of somebody from the garden: the figure of a man leaning with his back against the balustrade of the terrace."

"He would be facing the house?"

"Yes."

"About where would he be standing?"

I was beginning, despite myself, to like the police after all. The thing had a sheer intellectual fascination which was extraordinarily compelling. "It could not have been very far from this window."

"You could not identify the figure?"

"No."

"You made no further investigation?"

"No."

"And you saw no one else?"

"No one."

There was a silence. "This," said Appleby, "would be some five or ten minutes before Jane paid her first visit to this room and saw Sir Basil sitting at his desk." He turned to Leader. "Ring the bell."

Richards came and went. Jane, now somewhat recovered, came and went. And the upshot was that Jane, coming in to tend the fire, had been conscious of a fierce draught. Sir Basil, she said, liked the cold. In the coldest weather he would sit before an open window. Almost certainly the window had been open. About the curtains she couldn't say. Almost certainly they had been drawn or she would have noticed. But likely enough they had not been drawn completely. Sir Basil had a habit of interfering with drawn curtains, pulling them back a little to admit the air.

Appleby turned to me again as the door closed on the parlourmaid. "From where you stood on the terrace, and later in the garden, would you have been aware if the curtains here had been drawn back?"

"If they had been fully drawn back, yes; if there had been merely a substantial gap—even a foot or so—probably not."

"When Richards came in hard upon Jane's discovering Mr. Foxcroft they were just as they are now—a gap of a few inches. Just enough, if one stepped through the window from the terrace, to enable one to peer into the room." Appleby crossed to the desk and appeared to study the letter on margins. "Mr. Ferryman," he said, "you have given us an account of your movements. Will you now give us an account of something much more interesting?"

I looked at him in somewhat suspicious perplexity.

"I mean, will you now give us an account of your thoughts?"

"Really, Mr. Appleby—"

"I don't mean your thoughts since this thing has taken place, valuable though they would be. I mean your thoughts *before* it took place. For instance, what were you thinking of during your stroll in the park? It is for the purpose of reflection, as often as not, that one takes such a ramble." He paused and looked at me almost anxiously. "My point—my experience—is this. In any party of the sort gathered here—and particularly in a family party—there are likely to be various current issues and conjectures. Certain subjects are of general speculative interest. There is expectation here, apprehension there. Has Charles proposed to Mary—"

"Charles?" asked Leader perplexedly.

"And is Richard, perhaps, seriously ill?"

"Quite so," I said. It was evident that Appleby had developed a technique for putting things clearly to persons of low intelligence.

"The familial constellation," continued Appleby, as if suddenly remembering that I was in a different category. "If one can get hold of all that one is in a very strong position as an investigator. It is different, of course, if it is a matter of vanished spoons and forks. But in an affair like this the policeman has to seek very much the same preliminary information as the psychiatrist would seek were it he who was called in. It would often be better if it *were* he." And Appleby smiled at me encouragingly, like one excessively educated man to another. Leader, as if confident of what was to come, began vigorously to sharpen not one but several pencils.

The temptation was great. I do not know if I can construct a narrative or record a train of reflection. But to do so is my constant preoccupation. Moreover there was very little question of giving anything away; almost everything that I could tell I was very sure this young man would get at sooner or later. Still I might have hesitated but for the writer's primitive impulse to produce surprise. I turned to Leader: he poised his pencil. "In the park," I said, "I was meditating the rocket which my cousin Basil proposes to fire at the moon."

"The moon," said Leader with satisfaction. The exclusion of Saturn or Uranus might have been a considerable step forward.

"Or—in what is perhaps a better-authenticated version —my cousin's determination to establish a meteorological station in the antarctic. Whatever it be, he is proposing to sell Belrive."

Appleby, standing before the fire, was stuffing a pipe. "Your cousin," he asked, "is wealthy?"

"Not, I think, excessively so. This estate—of which the site must be extraordinarily valuable—is probably his principal asset."

"And he proposes virtually to sink it in his expedition: I see. What, by the way, of Mr. Foxcroft?"

"Wilfred is said to be something of a millionaire."

"And has no children?"

"He is unmarried. I suppose"—I saw no point in beating about the bush—"his brother Cecil would largely inherit. But my niece, Anne Grainger, who is his ward, might reasonably expect to be a legatee."

"And Sir Basil? His heir is his brother, Mr. Hubert Roper?"

"Yes."

I spoke a shade reluctantly and Appleby smiled. "There is nothing suspicious in being somebody's heir."

And before I could estimate the cogency of this soothing remark he went on: "So much for the main interest in all your minds: the Priory, it seems, is to be sold. What else?"

The direct appeal caught me. The young man was interesting and, though disconcerting, not unpleasant. The odd make-believe that we were colleagues—that my affiliations were here rather than in the library—held me for the moment. I talked—discreetly, but frankly on the whole. The substance I have already written down here. At least, I believe I saved the young man time. And I confess that I got some pleasure from the exercise.

CHAPTER XII

FROM THIS point—and for the remainder of this brief narrative—the reader will have to accept me as a sort of Watson. During the subsequent investigations Appleby appeared positively unhappy if I was not standing by at his side. During the interviews which he conducted with various members of the household he contrived that I should be present as what he called a family friend. And, again maintaining that a person so deeply researched in human character as myself was invaluable, he held conferences with me and made me a number of confidences in between. I suppose I knew that he was really up to something. But it was mildly exciting and I fell in with the role prescribed for me.

The interview with Basil I felt must be basically awkward. To ask a new acquaintance to dinner for the purpose of amusing one's sister and then to find him setting up as a detective officer in one's own study is a disconcerting experience. But Basil was not disconcerted. I think he summed Appleby up—and Basil could not have done what he had done were he not a sound judge of men —and liked him; continued to like him even when the interview became something of a duel and when it ended in the unaccountable way it did.

"Sir Basil," Appleby began, "has it occurred to you that you may be in some danger?"

Basil raised his eyebrows. "You alarm us," he said drily.

It was abundantly evident that Basil was not alarmed. But I admit that I had started at the suggestion, and his ironical glance was in my direction.

"You were working here at your desk at half-past seven; about fifteen minutes later somebody else sitting at the desk was sniped at through the curtains."

"Through the curtains?" Basil looked at the window-recess and frowned.

"The curtains were not just like that when you were in the room?"

"They were not. When I returned to work here after changing I found that they had been drawn to. At this time of year the servants pile up huge fires. Before sitting down I opened the french window and left the curtains a foot or so apart."

"They are not more than a couple of inches apart now. Can you suggest how that came about?"

"A few minutes after half-past seven, as you know, I went into the library. I wanted to be there when people began to assemble for dinner. It seems that Wilfred—Mr. Foxcroft, that is—then came in here to write a letter. It is likely that he would pull the curtains more or less to again."

"So that an assailant might have only an imperfect view of the person he was shooting at—a person sitting, notice, in his own light. Would you not agree then that you may be in some danger?"

Basil shook his head decisively. "No. I cannot conceive of anyone attempting a crime in such a haphazard way. If the shot was fired deliberately it is overwhelmingly probable that Wilfred was fired at. I am under no apprehension at all."

"Mr. Ferryman," said Appleby rat'ier enigmatically, "was persuaded to the contrary view." He paused. "Suppose, then, that Mr. Foxcroft was indeed deliberately shot: can you suggest any reason for such a thing?"

"It is conceivable that he came upon a thief, who fired in the course of making his escape."

"That is of course possible. . . . I think you must have been alone in the library when the shot was fired?"

Basil looked up quickly. "I was certainly alone. The others were rather late in coming down."

"And you heard nothing? Mr. Ferryman has suggested that there are so many traffic noises like the report of a revolver that a shot might pass unnoticed. But a shout or cry?"

"I heard nothing until the girl Jane began to shout in the hall."

Appleby paused again. Leader scribbled. "Sir Basil, can you think of anything in Mr. Foxcroft's circumstances which would make an attack of this sort likely? I am leaving out of account the notion of a burglar. It is improbable—if only because Mr. Foxcroft seems to have been shot as he sat."

"I can think of nothing. I am not well acquainted with his affairs."

"He is your nephew?"

"Yes."

"But you have never been closely associated?"

I began to wonder if I had done well in so obligingly sketching the family affairs. It was enabling Appleby fairly to gallop over the ground.

"We saw much of each other many years ago. We both climbed. But this is Wilfred's first visit to the Priory for a long time."

"There had been an estrangement?"

"In better English," said Basil in his driest manner, "there had been a quarrel."

Appleby nodded—nodded with his rather alarming air of momentary absence of mind. "Tell me," he said suddenly, "was anyone else who has recently been at the Priory in on all that—the climbing, I mean?"

"Only Ralph Cambrell, who was here at luncheon and with whom I had some business talk afterwards."

"Cambrell!" I exclaimed in surprise. "This is news to me. And I shouldn't have thought that he was at all that type."

"He was a different fellow before the mill caught him. Actually he and I climbed together only once. It was on Scafell and I took a horrid tumble on the ascent from Lords Rake."

For the first time that evening John Appleby showed something like emotion. "You had a tumble on Lords Rake!"

Basil smiled. "Just that. Cambrell was barely past scrambling; he would have been safe enough on Broad Stand. Central Buttress was about my mark then; in rock climbs I really hadn't so very much to learn. But tumble I did on Lords Rake and laid myself out. Cambrell had to stand by until I came to, and then we attracted the attention of some folk making for Pikes Crag. He behaved very properly and—I suppose because I don't greatly care for him—I have felt slightly awkward about it ever since."

"Pikes Crag," said Leader, and licked the tip of his pencil. It was absurd and I wanted to laugh. Instead I looked at Appleby and saw Appleby looking at Basil. The camera, it occurred to me, had become momentarily an x-ray machine; I have seldom received a more powerful impression of what is called a penetrating eye.

Abruptly—almost as if he were shaking off some compelling thought—Appleby stood up. "Sir Basil," he said, "may I go over the house?"

If Basil was either surprised or annoyed he did not show it. "Certainly—anywhere you like. We are very lucky that this wretched business has found you here" —he paused in a way that reminded me of Anne—"and so actively disposed."

"Thank you. And we must not keep you from your guests. Mr. Ferryman will perhaps show us around."

"Arthur," said Basil, "is just the man."

In the eighteenth century one expected to be able to see over any house when the family was not in residence; John Byng, in those Torrington Diaries which are favourites of mine, more than once expresses his indignation at being denied this prescriptive right of the gentleman traveller. I had often reflected that in the guise of an elderly housekeeper I would have made not a bad cicerone to Belrive. And now here I was landed with the job—and in circumstances which were odd and disturbing in an extreme. That I was just the man may have been true enough. But Appleby's interests, I supposed, could hardly be antiquarian, and I was quite at a loss to account for his suddenly expressed wish except in terms of the merest whimsy. Was he proposing to search for the missing weapon? It was scarcely a task to undertake at ten o'clock at night, and with a number of people still presumably waiting to give an account of themselves.

We moved into the deserted hall and Appleby wandered about as if he were in a museum, talking easily the while. "This party," he said, "was the occasion of a reconciliation between Wilfred Foxcroft and Sir Basil. A genuine reconciliation, let us suppose." He stopped before the Guardi. "Is this the picture your cousin has sold to Cambrell?"

"Yes."

Appleby looked at it doubtfully. "Do you think, Mr. Ferryman, that Guardi ever painted water with that square touch?"

I replied that I was without knowledge of Guardi's technique, but that I would not be at all upset if the picture proved a fake.

"In other words," said Appleby, "you dislike Cambrell too. Now, about that dispute which you say he had with your cousin. It is your impression that Sir Basil refused a favourable offer for his property. And that it was with reference to this refusal that Cambrell said—"

Leader flicked at his notebook. "*You damned fool, even your idiot paint-splashing brother would have more sense,*" he read.

Appleby nodded. "And that would be Mr. Hubert Roper, the heir to the estate?"

"Yes."

"Those are interesting family portraits. . . . Would you say that Cambrell's remark was sound?"

I considered. "No. I think Hubert would be most reluctant to sell Belrive at all."

"I see. But Cambrell may well be convinced that it is otherwise. . . . The Watts, I suppose, is of Sir Basil's father?"

I found this shilly-shallying between detection and connoisseurship depressingly reminiscent of Lucy at her most characteristic. Nevertheless I continued to feel that Appleby knew what he was about. I replied that the portrait at which we were looking was indeed of Basil's father.

"There is a strong family resemblance," said Appleby. "And it is in the Foxcrofts too. Both Wilfred and Cecil have a look of Sir Basil. And, incidentally, Wilfred and Cecil are astonishingly alike. They might almost be twins."

"Wilfred is the elder by about five years," I replied. I saw that in Appleby's observation—which was accurate enough—there might be found some food for thought. So presumably did Leader, for he made his inevitable note.

"I don't suppose," Appleby went on, "that there is a picture of Wilfred here? I have only seen him as a badly wounded man."

"There is none that I know of. Hubert is just beginning a portrait of Cecil—a fantastic affair viewed in a mirror and with some mildly improper emphasis on a woman's slipper. But that is beside the point."

Appleby looked at me doubtfully. "Yes," he said, "I

suppose so." He appeared to reflect. "I wonder if we might see it? I believe Leader would be interested. He does a bit himself."

I found it very hard to view this other than as a piece of the most unseasonable facetiousness. Nevertheless I led the way towards the attics. And Appleby continued to talk. "Dr. Foxcroft"—he was referring to Cecil—"is rather obviously a headmaster, is he not? I seem to remember him as a fellow of St. Thomas's. Does he keep up his scholarship at all?"

"I know nothing of his studies," I replied, "except that he reads Law's *Serious Call to a Devout and Holy Life*."

Even Leader made no note this time. The omission, curiously enough, was a mistake.

We had no business, I felt, in Hubert's temporary studio. But Horace Cudbird had even less. Yet there was Cudbird standing in the middle of the floor—standing in a sort of dogged perplexity which was emphasized by being caught and caught again in the three mirrors which were still in position. He looked up as we entered and greeted Appleby. "So here you are, John. I was wondering how long it would take you to drift up here." He turned to me. "John has always been one for the arts," he said. "I'm keener on photos myself."

"Mr. Appleby certainly appears to be an authority on Guardi's brush-work." I was unable to resist this stroke. For Leader was looking about him in a way that was far from suggesting that he did a bit himself. We had come up here as the result of the merest levity or the most irrelevant curiosity. But even as I concluded this

I looked at Appleby again and had my doubts. He was subjecting the room to the most serious scrutiny. "Photographs?" he said absently to Cudbird.

"Yes. And very instructive they can be." The brewer was looking at Appleby as one who sets a puzzle.

Appleby stopped looking about him. For the first time he looked as if he was really thinking hard.

"Particularly if one plays about with negatives and a scissors."

"Mr. Cudbird," said Appleby slowly, "do I understand that you feel in on this investigation?"

"You've got it, John. And if it weren't something improper with Wilfred Foxcroft lying at death's door, I'd put five shillings—"

"Never mind the impropriety," said Appleby briskly. "Done."

I looked at Leader. The disapproval on his face must have been a comical exaggeration of my own.

CHAPTER XIII

OF WHAT had happened in Basil's study there were eventually to be seven principal theories sponsored by seven different people—of whom one of the most emphatic was to be myself. But as I stood in Hubert's studio this was hidden from me, and I felt that Cudbird's proposal to import an amateur element into the investigation was in the most questionable taste.

"I feel a little unhappy," I said, "about intruding on Hubert's quarters in this way. So if Mr. Leader's artistic interests are satisfied—"

I broke off, compelled to silence by the extraordinary conduct of Appleby. He had been rummaging about among the sketches on the table in the most unblushing manner, and occasionally showing one to Cudbird as if he were setting a puzzle of his own. But now he had abandoned this and was delving into the painting materials near the easel. Among these were a number of bottles; each of these he picked up gingerly in turn, and sniffed at. It was just the way in which detectives are supposed to behave; the effect was enhanced when he produced a small magnifying glass and proceeded to scrutinise one largish bottle with the minutest care. "Of course," he said, "it depends on the powder and the weapon. But sometimes firing a single shot will get one's hand into quite a smoky mess. Turpentine is then useful." He put down the bottle. "The incriminating fingerprint, however, is not to be observed."

Somehow I felt suddenly depressed. The intellectual stimulation—the sense of a hunt going forward—had suddenly failed me. Instead, I saw an able and decently educated young man pursuing an undignified profession and proposing to involve Belrive in a great deal of scandal and embarrassment. At the same time I distinguished in myself a wholly irrational annoyance with Wilfred Foxcroft. It was callous; I wished him no ill; but I could not help feeling that it was just like him to plague us all by getting in the way of a mysterious bullet. I remembered his large confidence with the revolver as we drove up in the taxi; his informative prattle about safety catches and Verona drops. And even as I did so my mood changed. Suddenly I was thinking of Wilfred with a large benevolence and wishing for reassuring news from the hospital. As if to compensate for this again, the image of Cecil rose in my mind and I reflected what a very irritating and pompous creature Cecil was. I felt it rather a pity that it was not Cecil who had chosen to write a letter at Basil's desk. . . .

I came awake with a jerk. There was only one explanation of these vagaries, and it could be read on the face of my watch. When should we be allowed to go to bed? I had a horrid vision of these sniffings and prowlings and questionings protracting themselves into the small hours; of Belrive being given what Lucy calls "the works" and permitted no wink of sleep until all was discovered. I turned and addressed Appleby—raising my voice unnaturally, like a chairman determined to bring a straggling meeting to a close. "Since it is growing somewhat late—"

Appleby looked at his watch. "Yes," he said, "as it is growing quite late we may expect Wale to have got back. And he is the next person, Mr. Ferryman, with whom we must have some talk."

Desperation seized me. "Really, if you would excuse me—"

"These fashionable doctors feel they have to be very discreet. He will like to know that there is a witness on whom he may rely. Shall we go down?"

It was the merest blarney. But I gave in. We moved towards the door. Cudbird, who had been silent for some time, gave a last dogged look round. "I must be finding Sir Basil to say good-night," he said. "It was hardly right to stay, I'm afraid, being nothing of the family. Still, I can't help but take a real interest in Belrive now."

I halted. "Mr. Cudbird, are you going to buy the Priory?"

He looked at me in his rather wary way, suspicious of hostility. "It's very likely."

"Would it be unpardonable to ask what for?"

"A pub with a garden, a concert-hall, a skating-rink, a swimming-pool, a fun fair for the children, a creche, dancing, a workers' film society, a bit of a college." His eyes were sparkling as he reeled off this, to me, appalling catalogue. "Mind you," he said quickly, "there's money in it!" He looked from one to the other of us defiantly. "Make no mistake about that." He was gone.

Leader was looking bewildered. Appleby chuckled. "Out-and-out philanthropy. He'll spend thousands. And every old rascal in the town will say that Cudbird has gone soft at last."

"I think," I said, "that he might choose a more appropriate site for his rash social experiment."

Appleby crossed to a window and drew back the curtain. I suppose he could just see the intermittent glow of the great bottle licking the ruins which had once been the nerve centre of all the country round.

"It would not be wholly impossible," he said formally, "to maintain that you are mistaken."

We went downstairs. I was ruffled, as one can be when one sees a point without at all agreeing with it. Nothing pays less regard to sentiment than does sentimentality. And I could see only sentimentality in Cudbird's—and Basil's—plan; for the sake of an ephemeral "progressive" experiment it was going to obliterate all that was truly venerable at Belrive. It was no doubt because of the mood I was in that I found the ensuing incident peculiarly irritating.

We had nearly reached the hall—we were, in fact, just on the spot from which Lucy and myself had observed the Cambrell affair in the afternoon—when Appleby suddenly froze. The word is not too strong; his instantaneous, trained immobility put me in mind of those rather tiresome dogs employed to point at game. Involuntarily, I found myself behaving in the same way, and behind us Leader also came to a halt. We were spying on Cecil Foxcroft.

And Cecil seemed to be engaged in a somewhat similar activity himself. There was no one else in the hall; he was prowling round it much as he might prowl round a dormitory or changing-room when the boys were safely off on a run. The censor preparing to catch out the morally reprobate while warily apprehensive of being caught out himself; the proprietor ambiguously trespassing on what he has leased to others; the curious guest aware that curious servants may be round the corner: in Cecil all these displeasing suggestions were evident. When I first observed him he was trying the doors of a large glass-fronted cabinet. Having assured himself that they were unlocked he walked over to the fireplace and stood there a moment glancing round the hall—without, however, raising his eyes to the level at which we stood. Then he returned to the cabinet, opened it, and appeared to rummage within. The operation took perhaps a minute; when it was concluded he closed the doors again, made another survey of the hall, and moved off towards a second cabinet. I greatly disliked the whole thing and it was a relief when Appleby continued his interrupted progress downstairs.

We came up with Cecil just as he had opened the cabinet. It was an ancient and roomy Dutch affair, with iron-bound wooden doors. On the shelves were a number of large earthenware jars, painted with a variety of primitive designs in yellow and brown.

"Predynastic," said Appleby—more or less in Cecil's ear.

The boys had returned from their run distinctly out of time. Cecil's jump was a crumb of malicious comfort in the whole deplorable situation. Leader was still holding his notebook ritualistically before his stomach and had all the appearance of being about to demand an explanation of my cousin's conduct out of hand.

Cecil had recourse to severity. "Precisely. Undoubtedly of the Fourth Millennium, Mr.—um—Appleby. Such things should be under lock and key."

And Cecil put his spectacles on his nose and looked steadily at Leader. This, if I remember aright, is the standard scholastic technique for dealing with boys against whom no logical weapons are handy at the moment. But Leader was unimpressed. "Lock and key?" he said. "We're going to get more under lock and key than a heap of heathen pots." He gave the tip of his pencil a hungry lick.

Cecil frowned. "Property must be conserved. There has undoubtedly been an attempt at theft. Why else should Wilfred have been shot? And yet, when our energies should be bent on discovering what, if anything, has been stolen, Basil will do nothing at all. There is a vein of irresponsibility in Basil. Such carelessness"—he waved vaguely at the rows of Egyptian utensils—"is really a moral weakness. For if a man will not respect his own property how can we be assured that he will respect the property of others?" And Cecil, as if dimly aware of the dialectical weakness of this proposition, frowned very severely indeed.

"So you are endeavouring," said Appleby, "to make Sir Basil's moral weakness good?"

"I have been looking round. If anything important were gone I believe I should notice it."

It was not, I reflected, at all incredible. Cecil had that sort of mind. That his brother might at this moment be coughing out his life in hospital would not at all distract him from the sacred task of conserving property—even property which was presently to be dispersed in order to shoot rockets at the moon. The thing was an instinct with him. And I had a momentary fantastic vision. I saw Cecil, stuffed and in a glass case, standing in some museum of the future as an excellent specimen of Acquisitive Man. And this prompted me to say, absurdly: "The Guardi; Mr. Appleby entertains the gravest fears about that. It appears to be there still—but what if a copy has been cunningly substituted? Mr. Appleby—whose mind is a veritable *omne scibile*—doubts if Guardi ever painted water with that—ah—square touch."

Cecil looked at me suspiciously. "Substituted? One has heard of such things being done. Leonardo's Mona Lisa is said to be an instance. A remarkable picture." Cecil took his spectacles off again and turned to Leader. His expression became affable and instructive. "She is as old," he said, "as the rocks amid which she sits."

It was when our conversation had reached this pitch of inconsequence that Appleby chose to ask: "Dr. Foxcroft, would you be so good as to tell us what you were doing at a quarter to eight this evening?"

Cecil appeared to abstract his mind with an effort from Leonardo's masterpiece. "At a quarter to eight? I was in my bedroom."

"Just what were your movements from tea-time onwards?"

"I sat reading in the library until about half-past six. Then I went to my room and wrote letters. At about half-past seven I changed. I did not come downstairs until the disturbance in the hall."

"From half-past six onwards you did not leave your room?"

"That is so."

Cecil, it occurred to me, had suddenly turned into a model witness—brief and to the point. And even as this thought went through my head I heard the rustle of the leaves of Leader's notebook. "Dr. Foxcroft," he said, "we have had certain statements from servants." He paused heavily; his manner was very different from Appleby's. "And we have been told by the butler that at half-past seven he took a message to your room. He knocked twice, got no reply, and came away. How would you account for that now, sir?"

There was a pause and I glanced at Appleby. He was looking far from expectant. And Cecil's reply was brief and sufficient once more. "I was engaged," he said solemnly, "in prayer."

"Prayer," said Leader gloomily, and wrote.

"Meditation and prayer," amplified Cecil urbanely. "It is my habit at that hour."

There was a slightly embarrassed silence. Here, I thought, was something Lucy had never hit upon—a new sort of alibi and one difficult to shake. Not, for that matter, that Cecil could call his saints into court. . . .

We were interrupted by the glass door from the lobby swinging back. Sir Mervyn Wale came in, shaking a thin powdering of snow from an enveloping fur-lined coat. "Snow . . . mist . . . a hard frost," he said. "A wretched night for such adventures." He paused, glanced keenly at Appleby, turned to Cecil. "I got Badger," he said. "He's not what he was." Wale took off his coat and walked with it towards the fire. "Not a shadow of his old self, poor fellow." He spread the coat over a chair. "No one to touch Badger ten years ago, you know."

Cecil's features worked; they arranged themselves into an expression of decorous disappointment. "You mean, Wale," he asked, "that Badger has performed the operation on Wilfred with—ah—inadequate dexterity?"

"Inadequate fiddlesticks." Wale, like many fashionable physicians, had two manners: suave and brusque. The brusque was now well to the fore. "Never seen the thing done better. But slow. His record, you know, was—" As if remembering his exclusively lay auditory, Wale stopped, turned away, warmed his hands at the fire. "Fortunate we got Badger. Tell him what to do, of course. Must be off to bed. I'm past this sort of thing myself." He turned round and squared shoulders which were drooping with fatigue.

"There is hope, then, for Wilfred's life?"

"Hope? Of course there is. Serious, naturally. A close call. Deuced fortunate about Badger."

And Wale moved towards the staircase—competent, old, frayed, oddly abrupt. But my glance was all for Cecil. It was not often that he looked other than pleased with himself and with the world he adorned. I have remarked on his capacity for unawareness when stricture or satire was in the air. I have remarked that in primitive situations he would be dangerously without a sense of danger. . . . It was not so now. He was looking after Wale with consternation . . . with dismay . . . with terror open and declared.

CHAPTER XIV

WE WERE back in the study. Appleby had shown no disposition to pursue Wale for that interview in quest of which we had left Hubert's attic. Nor had he shown any further interest in Cecil. Indeed his interest in the household seemed to have evaporated for the time; Leader had been to the library and announced that police enquiries were over for the night.

"They're going to bed," said Leader, returning to the room. "I suppose we'd better—"

"Leader"—Appleby looked up from the brown study— "did you make a note of that book?"

"Book?" Leader was bewildered.

Appleby turned to me. "The book Dr. Foxcroft has been reading. Didn't you say it was Law's *Serious Call?*"

"Yes. Cecil has mislaid it. But I don't see—"

"That interview in the hall with Wale. Would you agree that Dr. Foxcroft was perturbed at the end of it?"

"Perturbed?" I said impatiently. "Cecil was terrified."

Appleby nodded. "That is no doubt what Sir Basil calls the better English of it. Terrified. Did you form any notion of the cause?"

I hesitated. "It is a dreadful thing to say, but what seemed to scare Cecil was Wale's announcement that Wilfred would probably recover."

"That's it." Leader interrupted with more animation than he had yet shown. "And we must make what we can of it."

"We must make what we can," said Appleby, "of this." He paused in some effort of recollection. " 'Hope? Of course there is. Serious, naturally. A close call. Deuced fortunate about Badger.' "

We stared at him.

"You see? *'Serious,* naturally. A close *call.'* Nothing could be plainer."

"You mean"—I found I had to struggle for words— "that Wale was making some covert reference to Law's book? It's perfectly fantastic. And Cecil would never pick such a thing up. He hasn't that sort of ear."

Appleby shook his head. "Nothing of that kind. And I don't suppose that Dr. Foxcroft *consciously* picked up anything. Wale used—quite by chance—the two elements in the title *Serious Call.* And that touched off some spring deep in Dr. Foxcroft's mind. Wale and the *Serious Call* were brought fortuitously together. And for Dr. Foxcroft their union somehow meant danger. That is the way, you know, that the mind works."

I was abundantly aware that the mind worked so. And though I considered Appleby's line of thought fantastic I looked at him with a new respect. It was plain that of every word that eddied around him he missed just nothing at all. I looked at my watch. "Really," I said, "that is a notion on which it would be well to sleep."

Appleby nodded. "Yes, and that is just what Leader here is going off to do. But I thought that you and I might take a stroll."

I must have looked at him much as the rabbit looks at

the snake. "A stroll?" I said.

"The nocturnal sort of which you are rather fond at the Priory. Leader, I shall be back in the morning. And I trust you to get me in on this officially. It interests me more and more."

The door closed on the departing Inspector Leader. "You know," I said, "I have seldom met a man less appropriately named."

Appleby smiled. *"Dux a non educando."*

The Latin was bad and our little joke not much better. But it established an atmosphere of something like companionship. Appleby filled his pipe again; I crossed to the desk and looked absently at Wilfred's letter on margins. "If my cousin recovers," I said, "or recovers sufficiently to talk, the affair will presumably explain itself."

"I doubt it. If somebody appeared at the window when the curtains were as Sir Basil left them—some feet apart— then no doubt Wilfred Foxcroft recognised his assailant. But if the curtains had been drawn to their present position and if the shooting was done through the resulting chink, then he may know no more about it than we do. Or even less."

"That," I said, "could hardly be."

It was a fishing remark, and Appleby recognised it as that. "We certainly appear to know very little. It is an unusually obscure case. The shot may have been fired by any one of a number of people. That is common enough. But it may also have been fired *at* any one of a number of people. Who thought to shoot whom? The problem has two unknowns." He moved towards the door. "I can't decently hang about much longer. But I would like that last prowl."

I followed him into the lobby; we put on coats; I found an electric torch. Outside it was snowing lightly. We stood for a few moments under the porch, watching the flakes eddying against a backcloth of darkness. Then we turned along the terrace towards the study window. Broad flags just powdered with snow were beneath our feet. Appleby scrutinised them carefully. Presently he straightened up, turned towards the house. I started as I noticed the posture he had taken up. He was immobile against the balustrading of the terrace; straight before him was a chink of light from the standard lamp still burning in the study. "The tram," he said, "threw out its flash of light, and here stood your man." He brushed the snow from the balustrade, sat on its broad surface and twisted round until he faced the garden. "And there"—a beam shot into the darkness from the electric torch—"is your lily pond. You would see the man, but scarcely the window. And this was at about twenty past seven. Sir Basil was still at his desk; the curtains still a foot or so apart. Your man could therefore see in clearly enough. But he would not himself be distinguishable from inside. Or merely as an unidentifiable figure taking a stroll. Twenty past seven. And nothing had happened by half-past, when Sir Basil left the library. Why the wait?"

"Obviously because Basil was not the quarry."

"Very well. Your cousin Wilfred comes in, goes up to the curtains and draws them nearly to." Appleby paused. "He could hardly do that without revealing his identity to your man outside—supposing your man—" He paused again. "Supposing your man is still there."

"We don't know that Wilfred did draw the curtains closer to. That may have been done by the assailant afterwards. Wilfred may simply have sat down and begun his letter."

"In that case again"—Appleby spoke with sudden decision—"the assailant knew whom he was shooting at. Only if he shot through a chink is it reasonable to suppose that he made a mistake. Try it now."

"Try it?"

"I'm going in again. Shoot at me through the present chink."

He was gone. And what he had meant by a last prowl was nothing less than a reconstruction of the crime. Once more I felt extremely indignant at the oblique fashion of this young man's proceedings. I had no fancy for playing at shooting Wilfred Foxcroft.

"Here I am." Appleby's voice came softly through the curtains. "I am at the desk with my letter before me. Fire ahead."

Rather uncertainly I stepped through the window and peered through the chink.

"Who am I?"

"You are the young man Basil asked to dinner. But only on scrutiny. If I had an *a priori* certainty that you were somebody else—"

"Precisely. Through the chink mistake is possible. But now this."

The curtains before me were pulled some eighteen inches apart—so suddenly that I jumped. Appleby turned to the desk. "Who am I now?"

"Appleby beyond question."

"Very well. Let us keep to your unknown man. He is out there, the curtains are back, he can see that it is Sir Basil who is sitting here. He waits. Sir Basil goes away. Wilfred Foxcroft comes in. If Wilfred Foxcroft drew the curtains closer he would be recognised as he did so. If he left the curtains as they were the same thing holds. Therefore if it was your unknown who did the shooting it was Wilfred whom he intended to shoot. For only if the assailant arrived on the scene *after* Wilfred had drawn the curtains to a chink would it be possible for him to make a mistake as to whom he was shooting at. Do you agree?"

I agreed. My head was in something of a whirl.

"But that is not quite watertight either. It holds only if your unknown were watching *uninterruptedly*. What about this? The unknown comes out on the terrace, looks in through the open curtains and sees Sir Basil working. Here is his chance. But he has no weapon. He hurries off to get one. And while he is away Basil leaves the room and Wilfred enters and draws the curtains closer. The unknown returns with his revolver. He takes it for granted that it is Sir Basil who has drawn the curtains and that it is Sir Basil whom he sees at the desk when he peers through the chink. He fires. What do you think of that?"

"I think," I said slowly, "that it gets you back to where you started."

Appleby frowned. "It gets me to this. Suppose your unknown did the shooting. Suppose he thought he was shooting Sir Basil. Suppose he really did go away as I have suggested to fetch a weapon, thus failing to realise that Wilfred Foxcroft had taken Sir Basil's place. Didn't fetching the weapon take a longish time? Your unknown was watching Sir Basil at about twenty past seven. Wilfred Foxcroft didn't enter the study until after half-past, and he had time to write a considerable part of a letter. The shooting can hardly have been before twenty to eight. Why did the unknown take twenty minutes to fetch a gun?"

"Perhaps because he went to fetch one from the range. To do that he would have to cross a good bit of the park."

"You were walking in that direction yourself?"

"Yes," I said. And added: "But I didn't fetch a gun."

Appleby ignored this touch of nerves. "How long would that take?"

"I really couldn't say with any exactness."

"Then it must be timed. In the dark, and with someone who knows the way. Would you mind?"

It was plain to me that Appleby just hated the idea of going home to bed. "Very well," I said. "Come along."

We went down the steps, our feet crunching on the snow. Cudbird's bottle winked and wobbled behind the ruins; street-lamps were still burning beyond the high wall of the park; elsewhere darkness was absolute. The garden was traversed in silence; we were well in the park itself before Appleby spoke. "I think we shall have company," he said.

I only half-gathered his words. My mind was back on the terrace, automatically retraversing all that I knew. "Company?" I asked stupidly.

The torch flickered over the snow before us. "Somebody set out on this expedition a little time ago. A woman. And I think—yes, she was followed by someone else."

There is nothing so wonderful in reading tracks in the snow. But I was in a condition of some strain and I had a sudden sense of Appleby as what Geoffrey had called him: a bloodhound unleashed. And of myself trotting at the creature's side.

"I think I ought to say"—the words came from me abruptly—"that I rather hate all this. I'm afraid I don't much believe in justice. So often we must punish in one man the deed that is born in another man's thought."

The snow fell softly on my face; I was very aware of the absurdity of thus tumbling out an obscure philosophical observation. But Appleby was interested. "Justice?" he said briskly. "No, I don't believe in that at all. Mind the branches."

I ducked; invisible twigs brushed my cheek. "But surely in that case—"

"I believe in injustice. That we are constantly in danger of committing it. And not merely in courts of law. Take this shooting." The voice was coming quietly out of the darkness. "Leader might make nothing of it. The queer, ugly thing that happened at Belrive that Christmas: it would be that to you all for the rest of your days. A family cupboard crammed with unjust suspicions. Much better clear it up."

"And you think you can clear it up?"

"Oh, yes. I have the key already."

It was extraordinarily cold in the park. But it was excitement, I think, which made me shiver at that moment.

"You have the key!" I cried.

"No." Appleby's voice was suddenly anxious. "I express myself badly. I know where the key is. Like the kettle at the bottom of the ocean. Not really lost." He laughed ruefully. "Wale said something that took me straight to it. Or all but. Anyway, it's gone again now."

I remembered Appleby's odd theory about the *Serious Call*. "Wale seems to have been uncommonly communicative," I said.

Appleby laughed again. "In an involuntary way. *Snow . . . mist.* That was what he said. It put me in mind of a poem."

"A poem!" I exclaimed—and wondered if Appleby was not as mentally tired as myself.

"Just that." There was a touch of mockery in his voice now. "He said something about snow and mist, and I thought '*Poem*,' and the key all but turned in the lock. Can you offer any suggestions?"

Cudbird's goblet filled and I got an uncertain glimpse of my companion's face. It was absorbed. His question was evidently seriously intended. For a few moments we walked in silence.

"What," I asked, "about this?

> *"Bolt and bar the shutter,*
> *For the foul winds blow . . ."*

"It sounds promising."

> *"Bolt and bar the shutter,*
> *For the foul winds blow:*
> *Our minds are at their best this night,*

And I seem to know
That everything outside us is
Mad as the mist and snow."

"No," said Appleby decisively, "it's not that. Something better known."

We trudged on in silence. To rummage through English poetry for mist and snow did not seem to me a promising way for a policeman to solve a shooting-mystery. But Appleby's mind must have continued to revolve round his odd problem. "Plenty of mist," he said presently, "in verse, and plenty of snow. But they can't often occur together. . . . We've been walking seven minutes at a slowish pace. Are we nearly—"

I felt his hand on my arm and realised that we were in darkness; he had switched off the torch. Instinctively I stopped. From somewhere just ahead, and in the shadow of the ruins, had come a sharp metallic sound. It was repeated once. Then there was silence.

For a full half minute we stood quite motionless, Appleby's hand still on my arm. And then with infinite caution my companion tiptoed forward. As if under irresistible compulsion I did the same. But I realised with dismay that we were spying once more.

CHAPTER XV

I SEE that I have reached the middle of my narrative as I have planned it. And for half-way house the nocturnal affair in the ruins serves nicely enough. It is dramatic without anything of the pitch of an inconvenient climax; it has *décor;* in some respects it is prelusive of the climax actually to come. Were I concerned—as is far from being the case—to dispose my materials with an anxious art I believe I should place this murky episode just where it stands now.

It took me by surprise. Appleby had remarked that we were to have company, but without rousing me to expectation. I was tired; I think I had fallen into that half-waking state which psychologists call hypnagogic; what I was chiefly aware of as I walked was a series of mental images of unusual vividness. Advancing upon the ruins, and with the slow flood and ebb of Cudbird's bottle before me, what I yet really saw was the window of Basil's study, its curtains parting and coming together as if marking the pauses in some enigmatic play. And at the same time another, and verbal, part of my mind was behaving in a similarly indisciplined fashion. The hunt for mist and snow had conjured up a memory of the hunt for Shakespeare's bells which Lucy had organised on the previous afternoon; scraps of quotation were running through my head again; I was in the poorest state of vigilance with regard to the outer world. It was in this abstraction, then, that I had felt Appleby's grip on my arm; that I had become aware of the reiterated metallic clatter in the ruins. It was from this that I was fully roused by a voice—Geoffrey Roper's—saying in the darkness: "Caught in the act!"

We had moved, stealthily, a few steps forward. Now we halted again. Geoffrey's voice had come from hard by the range; this much I knew though the bottle was out and the darkness whole. And I knew that he was speaking to Anne. The words had been spoken abruptly, almost with violence. But there was something in them still of a tone which Geoffrey kept for Anne alone.

The darkness flickered. A pinnacle, a buttress, a line of buttresses formed themselves high above us; green and acid light glowed through a crumbled clerestory window like the opening eye of some gigantic creature of the night.

Cudbird's Beers are Best. The faint green skin of light faded beneath a wash of madder; the ruins might have been a fragment of Burgon's Petra—the rose-red city half as old as time. The light ran down what I recognised as the wall of the lay dorter. Standing against it was a slim figure glimpsed momentarily as Anne's. "Why this impersonation"—it was Geoffrey's voice again—"of the Woman in White?"

"And why this impersonation of the Spy in Black?"

As if to cap the repartee, the invisible bottle tilted and the ruins dissolved in a whirligig of circling shadows. Then the beer came. A swiftly increasing amber flood, it at once lit up the scene and spread over it a mellow and golden patina; Anne in a long white cloak and Geoffrey in his dinner-jacket were revealed confronting each other across the wooden locker which constituted the armoury of the range. It was a theatrical piece. Appleby and I—unsuspected spectators—watched as from across an orchestra of fallen masonry and snow.

"If you must lurk," said Anne, "you should put on a coat. You're busy catching a cold, not me."

"What were you doing with that gun?"

I made a movement to break away from Appleby and reveal myself; even as I stirred, the great bottle snapped into darkness and the scene was gone. The darkness— a darkness of shadow and shifting violet penumbra— checked me, and I heard Anne's voice say: "Why was Wilfred so imperfectly shot?"

"Yes, Anne. Indeed, why?"

"I could give a guess."

"I could give a guess."

The acid green was flickering again above us. I re- alised with a shock that these young people carried their verbal affectations into their intimate talk—and into talk on a theme where they were surely out of place.

"We could give guesses." Rose turned to amber; they were standing as before with the golden-lit Priory be- hind them—like two modern folk strayed incongruously into a composition of Claude's.

"As could others."

"As could others—which is the point."

"Which is the point." The light faded on their unex- pected laughter. "But what were you doing with that gun all the same?"

"Till breakfast to guess."

"And is Cecil a liar?"

"Till breakfast to guess."

"To bed, then."

"To beds."

Green . . . rose . . . amber. They were gone.

"It took us nearly nine minutes," said Appleby. "But who would have expected such a treat at the end."

"I must say I don't at all like—"

"But I have eavesdropped and am, on the contrary, happy. And so to bed." Appleby chuckled. "Or, as Miss Anne so precisely puts it, to beds."

"I hope," I said, "that you make something of what you have heard." The coolness with which Appleby carried off our deplorable conduct exasperated me slightly.

We moved over to the locker by which Geoffrey and Anne had been talking. "I admit," said Appleby, "that their idiom stands a little in need of interpreting. But I have no doubt you can do that." He halted and flashed the torch. "Locked, as it certainly ought to be. The young woman came with a key and under cover of darkness returned a revolver to its place. The young man followed her. One might see the expedition as implying guilt. But I felt that it might very well be a matter of giving a suppressed sense of melodrama an airing. As they said: Woman in White and Spy in Black."

We were retracing our steps across the park and a light night wind was now blowing the snow in our faces. My instinct was to get Appleby off the premises and crawl to bed. Nevertheless I could not resist an impulse to continue the debate. "Anne had some plan to fire off a revolver up in the gallery—a plan which Basil vetoed. She may have brought the revolver up to the house for that, and felt after the shooting that it was an embarrassing thing to have about. Her method of returning it would be melodrama, as you say."

"I gathered that she and Geoffrey Roper were not accusing each other; their clipped talk was a sort of review of possible accusations from elsewhere. And more was meant than met the ear."

"They talk," I said, "in a very affected way."

"No doubt. But—do you know?—they remind me a little of the people in your books."

I said nothing. It was a piece of detection which I did not relish.

"Which is a compliment to them, of course. They can play that verbal game only because they are exceptionally aware both of each other and of the world around them. Of the possibilities in this shooting—of how this or that may be made of it—they are likely to be masters. And they have certainly penetrated to the very heart of the mystery."

"Perhaps," I said, "they are better up than we are in mist and snow."

Appleby laughed. "That, as you know very well, is simply a matter of a lost association in my own mind." His voice became serious and convinced again. "I say they touched the very centre of the thing."

We walked in silence, the torch picking out our path. Behind us Cudbird's bottle had given over for the night; the cessation of its flicker on the snow before us made the night feel colder than before.

"Can I get out," Appleby asked, "without coming back to the house?"

I told him that there was a sort of postern near by which would take him out on the main road; we turned off our path and found it without difficulty. "A Yale lock," said Appleby; "but not locked. So at night anyone may stroll into the park?"

"You will find that, though the tram line is hard by, this actually gives on a little *cul-de-sac*. It is so quiet that I suppose nobody troubles about locking up. Turn to the right and you will come to the main road just opposite Cambrell's mill."

Appleby put his hand on the latch. "How simple," he said, "for Cambrell to slip in here and do any shooting required."

"No doubt." I was somewhat startled at the casual manner in which Appleby threw out this suggestion.

"Well, I must be off." He opened the door. "By the way, *is* Cecil a liar?"

This nicely contrived change of theme had its effect; the torch jerked in my hand.

"Geoffrey Roper asked that. Is Cecil a liar? And perhaps that is where you can interpret. To what would he be referring?"

I hesitated. Here was something that I had refrained from communicating to Appleby earlier. And in this chilly situation I scarcely felt like it now. But I saw that—whatever my own belief—it was something which Appleby would not consider irrelevant to his investigation. Which meant that he would get at it himself sooner or later. "I think," I said, "that I can give a guess."

Appleby said nothing. But he closed the door. I had extinguished the torch. We might have been in a darkness calculated for purposes of the confessional.

"Wilfred, as you know, is Anne's guardian; originally he was joint-guardian with my father. He has always been the business man of the family. But he was, of course, somewhat too young to be a suitable person to act alone."

"I see."

"When my father died no further arrangement was made. Ann had no property of her own; her future was largely a matter of the discretion of her wealthy remaining guardian."

"So much I've gathered."

"There is really nothing more except Cecil's gossip. I am afraid Cecil's feelings for his brother Wilfred are unkindly. The other evening he took me for a stroll in the park here and confided to me that he did not consider Wilfred's relations with Anne—or rather his intentions towards her—as at all proper."

"And that, I take it, does not cover a desire on Wilfred's part to marry his young ward?"

"Cecil assures me that Wilfred is a confirmed bachelor."

I thought I heard what might have been a sigh come from Appleby. "Only let somebody be shot," he said, "and this sort of stuff comes up. What is your own opinion of the business?"

I hesitated. "Anne has a mocking way with her. Once or twice she has hinted at Wilfred's burdening her with unwanted sentiment. But a guardian who is perfectly properly disposed may be slightly jealous of his ward's suitor. And if ward and suitor consider themselves entitled to some sort of settlement from him out of hand friction may easily grow up. The resulting situation I can imagine Cecil misconstruing readily enough."

"Anne, in fact, being due to tell Geoffrey that Cecil is a liar indeed."

"Yes. It is very distressing to have to explain all this."

"I am grateful to you for keeping nothing back. . . . Good-night."

He was gone. And as I returned to the house I found myself wondering if there had been something faintly mocking in his voice.

CHAPTER XVI

BREAKFAST on the following morning was an unusually punctual affair. That this was due to our having slept soundly seems unlikely: most of us, indeed, showed signs of a contrary experience. Nor was much appetite evident. Curiosity was the motive which brought the house party so promptly round Basil's eggs and bacon. And of this curiosity I was myself the centre.

I can see now that Appleby had thought this out. He had affected to enlist me as an assistant on the ground that I possessed more than common insight into human character. Actually, he was proposing to use me as a sort of long-handled spoon. His technique consisted largely in a vigorous stirring-up of the human elements in his problem. And he stirred with me.

The choice was not without art. People of my sort—imaginative workers in rather a wire-drawn kind—are commonly an unhappy mingling of difference and ability. We tend to sit in a corner and feel that our talents entitle us to a larger share of attention than we get. Not content to rest in the consciousness of a respectable fortune in the bank, we have an itch to make a show by jingling the loose change in our pocket. To receive some attention not for what we printed last year but for what we are saying and may be thinking now: this is something under which we expand. I fear I expanded more than was discreet.

Hubert Roper was the first person to speak. "Cecil," he said disapprovingly, "you've changed colour."

Geoffrey looked up from a plate of porridge. "Interesting, isn't it? Greenish tones showing through. He reminds me of the doubtful Vermeer at Brussels."

It was certainly true that Cecil had turned pale, though an untrained eye had to take the greenish tones on trust. He crumbled a piece of toast and gulped coffee with an effort, an altogether different man from the Cecil who had been taking roast duck in his stride the day before. Whether he would have replied to the badinage directed at him did not appear, for Hubert had now turned to his sister Lucy. "You look off colour too, my dear. Those tiresome policemen, no doubt, ignoring all the principles of the craft. Don't your sleuths exhaustively question everyone on the spot? But except for Arthur here and a word with Basil those fellows last night took no interest in any of us."

"A most mistaken impression." I spoke abruptly, so that everyone swung round. Hubert Roper was a person for whom I had never entertained very strong feelings either of dislike or approval; at this moment, however, he had aroused considerable irritation in me. "Basil's new friend Appleby is a most pertinacious young man and takes the liveliest interest in us all. Your studio, Hubert, quite absorbed him."

"My studio! What the devil do you mean?"

"He inspected it on the pretext that his colleague Leader is something of a connoisseur. He sniffed at your bottles much as if you had been the Borgias' poisoner, and as for your sketches—well, he studied them as if they might prove the cardinal documents in the case."

It would be idle to deny that I enjoyed the sensation which this revelation caused. I had an irresistible impulse to cap it with another. "Cudbird was interested too. I believe there might be a commission or two in him when it comes to decorating"—my eye went to Basil at the head of the table—"his skating-rink, his fun fair, his creche—"

"His concert-hall," said Basil drily, "and his *maison de dance*. I have been afraid, Arthur, that all that might be a blow to you. But, for what I am after, it seemed the best way."

"A blow?" said Anne. "At the moment Uncle Arthur seems less contused than contusing. Hubert staggers."

It was true that Hubert appeared startled. "Cudbird?" he said. "Has that little tyke been up in the attic too?"

"Yes. Although he confesses that his taste is rather for the photographic. He associates photographs in some way with last night's wretched affair. His precise line of thought is obscure to me—as are a good many other things. But I am convinced that Appleby hopes to clear up the whole affair in time."

"As for the interrogations Hubert hankers after," said Basil, "I don't doubt they will take place to-day. I expect Leader back at any time—and Arthur's young friend as well. Unless, of course, Arthur has been left in charge."

"Am I mistaken," asked Geoffrey, "in distinguishing a doggy smell in this room now? After all, Arthur was virtually kennelled with the bloodhound for hours on end."

"Not entirely kennelled, Geoffrey," I said. "We took the air."

Geoffrey looked blank, but Anne's eyes narrowed. "Is it conceivable," she asked, "that Uncle Arthur also takes the biscuit?"

I recognised this as a fair enough description of my conduct in the ruins some nine hours before. "It would not be an exaggeration," I replied, "to say that I fairly took the cake. I mean"—I looked round the table—"that I helped Appleby to eavesdrop on Geoffrey and Anne. A somewhat barren discussion of their riddling talk followed."

This time the table was stupefied. But I do not think that I was now talking for effect; it seemed to me that the least I could do was to be reasonably frank.

"The doggy smell," said Hubert, "seems to be about the mark."

I flushed. "You needn't think that I am eager for a blood-hunt. Far from it. Wilfred, I hope, will recover and the whole thing be forgotten. Or forgotten by everyone but the perpetrator of last night's folly."

"Folly?" said Sir Mervyn Wale. He was evidently in his blandest mood again, and now spoke for the first time. But mild as his interjection was, I noticed that it made Cecil start.

"Folly," I repeated. "Criminal folly, if you like. I believe the memory of it will be"—I hesitated—"will be punishment enough. I see little sense in any of us going to prison."

There was silence. My auditory was shocked. It was also a little impressed.

"I cannot agree with you," said Wale presently. "These Tolstoian positions ignore the brute fact of bent and habit. Repentance and amendment *might* follow. But more probably what would follow would be a second attempt. Foxcroft"—he turned to Cecil—"does your experience with youth not bear me out?"

Cecil's reply was inarticulate; I had the impression that he had gulped coffee the wrong way down. And Geoffrey interrupted Wale's speculative excursion. "Tolstoian or not, the fact remains that Arthur chummed up with the hound and went padding about. And we are all agog to know what happened."

I shook my head. "Very little happened. We reconstructed the crime—"

Lucy Chigwidden put down her cup with a clatter. "Really, Arthur, it makes me feel quite queer. I have so often—"

"*A single pistol-shot,*" said Geoffrey, "*rang through the startled hall:* will this at least cure Lucy of all that? It would be nice to feel that Wilfred's sacrifice had not been in vain. Why not try historical fiction, Lucy? You could always let off a musket or matchlock if you felt a trick of the old rage. A single bombard reverberated in the base-court; a blunderbuss boomed in the buttery."

"We reconstructed the crime," I repeated, "and prowled about. There was some tentative exploring of alibis. For instance, I had gone out for a stroll—no alibi at all. Cecil was engaged in prayer."

"Prayer?" said Anne. "One feels that if Cecil prayed one would hear him at it. Sir Mervyn, had you joined him?"

Wale smiled a very properly chilly smile. "I was resting in my room. Another instance of what Ferryman calls no alibi at all. It is to be hoped that in the course of his devotions Dr. Foxcroft didn't forget *you*."

Geoffrey Roper's chuckle was interrupted by Cecil. "Basil," he said loudly, "I am sorry to say that I have to leave." He held up a letter which had been waiting for him on the breakfast table. "A conference." He stuffed the letter in a pocket. "An important conference which I dare not miss."

"A chilly time of year for conferences," said Wale. "Where is it to be held?"

Cecil took another gulp of coffee. "There is some—ah—last-moment doubt. I shall receive a telegram at—um—Crewe."

"Cecil," said Anne, "has had a very Serious Call."

Abruptly, Cecil set down his table-napkin. "I shall pack while you are finishing breakfast."

We stared at him in astonishment. "Do I understand," asked Basil, "that you are proposing to go away leaving no address?"

"What about my picture?" demanded Hubert.

"And what," said Anne, "about the police? If they can't prevent his going they will certainly have him shadowed. Wherever Cecil travels he will be followed by a large man in a bowler hat. A 'tec. Observation will pursue him in his most intimate moments. The 'tec will watch and Cecil will pray. Or perhaps the police will employ Uncle Arthur once more."

"It would be most injudicious," said Basil. "I hope, Cecil, that you will be able to change your mind."

Cecil sank back in his chair. Whatever terror possessed him, I think it was overborne by the prospect of being followed about by a man in a bowler hat. Presently a thought seemed to strike him. "A lawyer," he said. "Basil, I want a lawyer; have you a lawyer here?"

"Certainly I have. Man named Cotton."

"In the telephone book?"

"Of course. Clement Cotton. Firm is Cotton and Cotton."

At this Cecil sprang up and retreated in the oddest backwards fashion from the room—much like one of his own charges having reason to apprehend a kick on the behind. In the baffled silence which followed his voice could be distinguished speaking urgently in the lobby. "He's got on to Cotton," said Geoffrey. "One wonders is what on?" He laughed confidently at his jingle.

Wale stood up. "We must have Beevor," he said with conviction.

"Beevor?" Basil, who was addressed, looked somewhat blank. It took a lot to move Basil's masterful calm, but I think he was beginning to feel the situation as getting beyond him.

"I ought to say that I have been Dr. Foxcroft's medical attendant for some time. Now he appears to have lost confidence in me. But before resigning the case I consider it my duty to call in Beevor. With your permission, Roper, I will go to the study."

So while Cecil summoned Cotton, Wale summoned Beevor. The rest of us remained in the breakfast-room in a silence which was presently broken by a sniff and a sob. It was Lucy Chigwidden. She had begun quietly to cry. "I can't understand it," she said; "I just can't understand a single thing!" She put a handkerchief to her eyes and composed herself. "You must forgive me, Basil; but it really is very upsetting indeed. So bewildering *all round*. . . ."

I realised that Lucy's professional vanity was mortified. The mystery which surrounded us she was as little able to penetrate as anyone else.

There was another pause. "The relationship between this Wale and Cecil," said Hubert, "has been problematical from the first. For who would cleave to Cecil? The puzzle is there."

"And yet," said Anne, "Wale undoubtedly clave. *Venus tout entière à sa proie attachée* is about the measure of it. But we neglect the narrative of Uncle Arthur."

We do not greatly uncle and aunt in our family; I regarded Anne's Uncle Arthuring me as an irritating affectation. "My dear Anne, there is little narrative to give. Appleby detected you returning a revolver to the range; he listened to your talk with Geoffrey; he made certain acute observations upon your character; and then he went away."

"Returning a revolver?" said Basil with severity. "Anne, what is this?"

"Please, I brought a revolver up to the house to play a joke on Lucy. After the shooting I felt it might be an awkward companion, so I took it back. Geoffrey followed me and I promised to explain at breakfast. Now I'm explaining. Of course I know"—she mimicked Basil outrageously—"that it was most injudicious."

I have always felt slightly responsible for Anne; it was my instinct now to say something by way of diversion. "Appleby," I remarked, "is acute and pertinacious. But in one or two particulars he seemed to me to lack discretion. I have mentioned that we came upon Cudbird in Hubert's attic. He and Appleby—they appear to be old acquaintances—exchanged somewhat enigmatic observations. And then—if I am not mistaken—they made some sort of bet as to who would get at the truth of the matter first. I could see that Leader disapproved."

Basil—whose reactions were often unexpected—laughed for the first time since the shooting. "My dear Arthur," he said, "do you know that in your composition there is a touch—just the faintest touch—of Cecil? Lurking in you is the feeling that certain things are not done." He paused. "Priories, for instance, are not sold." He looked at me quizzically. "But consider this affair on its merits. Appleby wants the truth. Cudbird, who is a clever fellow with the instinct of scientific curiosity, is moved to hunt for the truth too. Why should they not spur each other on with a bet? If they had wagered, say, on the chances of Wilfred's recovering I would be prepared to join Leader in disapproving heartily. Of Wilfred's fight they can only be spectators. But in solving the mystery they can be *agents*. That makes all the difference."

There were times, I reflected, at which Basil could be distinctly heavy. "A difference isn't necessarily the same thing as all the difference," I said. "And, anyway, I repeat that Appleby seems to me not altogether discreet. He shows his hand. For example, I showed him out last night by the little door opposite the mills. As a result he revealed the way his suspicions were turning."

"There!" said Geoffrey. "I knew we should get something out of Arthur at last."

"He remarked how easily the shooting could have been done by—"

Richards appeared at the door. "Mr. Cambrell," he announced.

CHAPTER XVII

HARD upon Richards' announcement came Cambrell himself. "Roper," he said, "will you forgive me for coming in at this hour? I felt I had to say how very sorry I was to hear your bad news." And Ralph Cambrell pulled a long face. He pulled it, I thought, without much difficulty, as if the ribbon and tape business were going through a lean time.

Basil's acknowledgments and report of the last news of Wilfred were accompanied by the rustle of a newspaper down the table. It was Anne. "But it's not in the *Post*," she said. "However did you get to know?"

Cambrell looked embarrassed. "The police," he replied. "I had it from the police. The fact is"—he turned again to Basil—"that I have explanations to make." He hesitated. "And something to return." He took a book from under his arm and laid it on the table.

"Have a cup of coffee," said Basil.

Cambrell looked more disturbed still. "And of course an apology to offer. I beg you to forgive what I said at our parting yesterday afternoon."

We looked uncomfortably down our noses. Basil admirably contrived not to be brusque and not to be hearty; Cambrell got his coffee, got two lumps of sugar. "Yes," he said; "as I say, the police. They appear to be quick-working and efficient. That is most satisfactory."

"Most satisfactory," said Anne.

"Most satisfactory," said Geoffrey.

Cambrell shifted slightly on his chair. "The book. They traced me through the book I left in your study."

Basil looked puzzled. "I am quite sure you didn't—"

"The book I left last night."

"The book," said Geoffrey and Anne in chorus, "he left last night."

Basil, I am glad to record, stood for no more of this. "Anne," he said, "Geoffrey, no doubt you have your own plans for the morning."

The door closed on the impossible couple. Cambrell looked slightly relieved. "I had better begin at the beginning. After leaving you yesterday afternoon I went across to the office and worked late. A little after seven o'clock I prepared to go home. Then it occurred to me that in the matters we had been discussing the—the last word had not perhaps been said. I remembered your remarking that you would probably be working in your study till dinner. So I slipped into the park by the little door—"

Basil's eyes flickered for a moment towards mine. I could see that he knew very well what I had been about to report when our visitor was announced.

"—and strolled up to the house. The front door was open—"

"Yes," I interrupted. "I left it open when I went out."

"—and the hall deserted. I noticed that it was a couple of minutes after half-past seven. I had an impulse—I am afraid it is most inexplicable—not to present myself to your servants again in a formal call. So I walked straight down the little corridor, knocked at the door of your study, and went in. It was empty."

Basil no more than faintly raised his eyebrows. "I see. I had just left it. And Wilfred had not yet gone in. I am sorry I missed you."

Cambrell received this irony unresentfully. "I waited for a couple of minutes. I must tell you that I had with me a circulating-library book which I was taking home. I must have laid it down on the desk." Cambrell paused. "I say I waited a couple of minutes. But perhaps it was really less than one; in fact it didn't take me long to realise that I had done an exceedingly awkward thing."

"Quite so."

"You will not think it absurd when I say that a mild panic seized me. I picked up my book, returned to the hall, found it still deserted, and left the house, closing the door behind me. Only in my flurry I took the wrong book."

"Odd," said Basil. "If you had wanted to demonstrate your presence in the study you could scarcely have left a better clue."

"No doubt. And as I say, the police acted most expeditiously. They noticed my book when examining the room and had the thoroughness to ask your butler if you subscribed to this particular local library. He told them that you had books sent down from London. So they roused the manager of the book-shop in the small hours of this morning, examined his files and traced the book to me. A young detective officer called Appleby—a very civil fellow—was on my doorstep at eight this morning and I had to explain the whole thing. He was very reasonable and seems to agree that I acted unwisely but naturally enough." Cambrell announced this with some satisfaction, seemingly unaware that in Appleby's pronouncement a certain judgment of character was involved. "And then I felt, of course, that I must come over at once and explain everything. And return the book I took away with me."

Basil picked up the volume from the breakfast table. "Yes," he said, "I see. Law's *Serious Call*."

Crossing the hall some twenty minutes later I met Geoffrey. Clad in a large sweater and muffler, he was swinging a badminton racket. "*This sight of death*," he said, "*is as a bell That warns my old age to a sepulchre.* You remember Wale quoting that in Lucy's game? I was going to draw something surrealist on it this morning. But the fingers get too cold this weather. So if the sleuths come Anne and I are in the coach-house. And Cecil is locked in his bedroom."

"Locked in his bedroom?"

"I mean he has locked himself in. As you know, Wale has been Badgering one Beevor. Quite a Bestiary in that." Geoffrey paid this the tribute of a long, loud laugh. "But Cecil will neither be Badgered nor Beevored. In fact he's rapidly developing an anti-medical mania. No one is to be let in to him except this lawyer he's sent for. Odd, isn't it? As Lucy would say, the plot thickens. Sickens would be the better word, to my mind. Off to who-goes-with-whom, I suppose?"

This was Geoffrey's name for my sort of writing. His generation affects to be uninterested in personal relations and to regard every drawing-room as a boring bedroom in disguise. "Yes," I said, "I shall try to do a little work, and it will be about people who are reasonably aware of each other. By the way, Appleby thinks that you and Anne are not unlike the creatures in my books."

Geoffrey stared; I think he was really shocked.

"He thinks of you as exceptionally well up in who-goes-with-whom—in the whole wash and drift of feeling at Belrive. He also remarked that you have penetrated to the heart of the mystery."

"If he means that I see there *isn't* a mystery, he's right."

"Isn't a mystery? I hardly think he meant that."

Geoffrey opened round eyes on me. "Surely *you* don't think there's any doubt about who shot Wilfred?"

I looked at him in dismay. "Really—"

"Basil shot Wilfred, of course. Tried to murder him. When the bed-stuff bores you come and watch the mad-minton."

And my young kinsman shrugged his shoulders and moved off. But after a couple of paces he turned round. "Do you imagine"—he spoke with something between irritation and vehemence—"that a chap like Basil would let a fat little banker stymie something *serious?*"

The tail-end of this shocking conversation Basil might almost have heard; he came into the hall just as Geoffrey disappeared. Simultaneously Richards emerged; there had been a summons to the front door. A moment later he reappeared, ushering in first Inspector Leader, and then an elderly man of substantial and severe deport-ment, accompanied by a nondescript person carrying a despatch-case.

"Sir Basil," said Leader, "Mr. Foxcroft is now out of

danger, I am glad to say."

The substantial person handed Richards an overcoat. "Excellent," he said. "We are devoutly thankful. But I presume he will want my hastily summoned service all the same—eh, Sir Basil? And good-morning to you."

"Good-morning, Cotton. You haven't got the situation quite clear. The inspector here is referring to Wilfred Foxcroft, who is in hospital after being shot last night."

"Shot? Dear, dear." Cotton moved abruptly away from Leader, as if dissociating himself from one suddenly revealed as a natural enemy. "Shot, indeed. Well, we mustn't start talking about it here. When that sort of thing—ah—begins to happen discretion is the word. But I understood that someone called Foxcroft—"

"Wilfred's brother Cecil. He has decided that he requires legal advice in a hurry and I gave him your name."

"Odd," said Cotton. "I came in a hurry because I gathered it was an urgent matter of a will. Tripet, was it not a will?"

The nondescript person nodded. "Yes, sir. A will, certainly."

"A will," said Cotton, "to be drafted urgently. So I brought Tripet. You won't believe me, but I've known testators determined to leave legacies to everyone within thre miles round. Virtually impossible to find a witness. So I bring Tripet. Eh, Tripet?"

"Yes, sir."

Basil was watching Richards out of the hall. "I have no doubt my nephew Cecil wants to make a will. But I ought to tell you that he is thought to be unwell. His doctor, Mervyn Wale, is staying with us, and has just proposed to call into consultation a colleague called Beevor."

"Beevor?" exclaimed Cotton. "Beevor's an alienist. Tripet, isn't that right?"

"Yes, sir."

"Come along then, man—come along. No time to be lost. Would it be any use taking instructions on testamentary dispositions from a client after Beevor had been at him—eh? Use your sense, Tripet."

"No, sir. Certainly, sir."

"I understand," I said, "that Dr. Foxcroft has suddenly developed an unreasoning dread of the medical profession. The trouble is there."

"It only sounds sense to me. To my mind consulting doctors is either a waste of money or a forlorn hope. Eh, Tripet?"

"No, sir; I can't say I agree."

"Quite right, Tripet, quite right. Know your own mind. Essential in the law."

"Thank you, sir. Yes, sir."

Leader shifted his feet in discreet impatience. "Sir Basil, if you could spare the time—"

Basil nodded. "Arthur, could you take Cotton and Mr. Tripet up to Cecil? It is distressing and absurd, but it appears that he is reluctant to come down."

I led the way, wondering as I did so what had become of Appleby. He must have worked through the small hours on the matter of the circulating-library book. Perhaps after interviewing Cambrell he had gone to bed. Perhaps in the investigation of the Belrive affair he was going to take what might be called the night shift.

Cecil's room was at the end of a corridor. I tapped at the door. "Cecil, here is Mr. Cotton, the solicitor whom you asked to call."

There was a sound which was distinguishably that of a heavy piece of furniture being moved. "Ask him," came Cecil's voice, "if he has a card."

I glanced rather uncomfortably at Cotton in the half-light of the corridor. "I'm afraid," I murmured, "that he does seem to be in an eccentric mood."

"And be so good as to push it under the door."

Had Cecil spoken wildly or in agitation the situation would have been distressing enough. But the voice which was coming to us was very much that of the headmaster on his own ground—calmly authoritative, intimidatingly august. And this imported an uncanny element into the affair.

Cotton produced a card and handed it to Tripet. Tripet pushed it under the door. It disappeared with a nervous jerk. After a moment's pause came the sound of a key turning in the lock. There was another and longer pause and we were told to enter. Cecil had retreated to a little writing desk at the far end of the room. He rose and advanced towards Cotton with measured cordiality. He might have been receiving a parent of respectable but undistinguished condition. "Mr. Cotton?" he said. "How do you do?" And at the same time he looked rather apprehensively at Tripet's despatch-case. He was speculating, I believe, on the chances of its really harbouring stethoscopes and clinical thermometers. "It is my desire," said Cecil—and he spoke with even more of an eerily false calm—"to make a will."

Cotton bowed. "Always a wise resolution, my dear sir," he murmured soothingly. "The obligation to make exact testamentary dispositions—"

"Quite so." Cecil's pupils narrowed, as if he were peering into the remote past. "Property must be conserved. I commonly give a little talk—" He broke off and looked carefully round the room. "But at the moment it is not property that is in my mind. My directions concern disposal"—he hesitated—"concern disposal of the remains."

I gave a start, and in doing so knocked a book off a small table. Cecil positively jumped. "Arthur," he said, "be so good as to pull the chest of drawers against the door."

"My dear Cecil, can I not persuade you—"

"It breaks the draught. On these chilly mornings I find it breaks the draught."

I did as I was bidden.

"—of the remains. And to this I wish to give legal effect at once."

"A statement of wishes," said Cotton smoothly, "formally witnessed. An excellent thing. But I must tell you that you have actually no power—"

"And there must be two copies, made *immediately*. And, Arthur, one of these I desire you to take down to the hall and pin up."

I stared at him. "*Pin up?*"

"Pin up. Pin up." Cecil's calm had gone. He was trembling violently. Suddenly he sat down on his bed. "A little talk," he said. "I give a little talk. On what I call Control . . . what I call Control . . . *Control*. . . ."

CHAPTER XVIII

GOING downstairs—for I had concluded that Cecil's distresses might decently be regarded as none of my business—I found Lucy Chigwidden domestically employed in the hall. On a table before her were masses of shaggy chrysanthemums, and these she was beginning to arrange in bowls. Beside her also was a large sheet of paper on which she was making spasmodic scrawls with a pencil. "Arthur," she called out, "come and help me with your advice. I am arranging the flowers because it is so soothing." She made a jab at her paper. "How beautiful these roses are."

"My dear Lucy, you are arranging chrysanthemums."

Lucy peered in mild surprise at the massed flowers. "Dear me—indeed I am! Do you know, I was expecting them to bring roses—Andrews promised roses—and so I *saw* them as roses. And now I am quite disappointed. But it shows what Doctor Johnson calls the prevalence of imagination."

Lucy was determinedly literary. "It shows," I said, "great absence of mind. And that pencil is unsuitable for cutting stalks; you will find the scissors on the table more convenient."

"Thank you, Arthur." Lucy picked up the scissors and poised them over her paper. "I suppose I *was* in something of a brown study. I am beginning to work it out."

"Better a brown study than a blue funk—which is the condition in which I have just left Cecil."

"Ah!" Lucy, who had crossed the hall to ring a bell, placed a finger on her lips. "Richards, take this bowl to the library. For the large window."

"Lucy, you are incorrigible. Richards is the butler. That young person who has just gone out is called Rose."

"Richards rose abruptly," said Lucy.

"I beg your pardon?"

"*Richards rose abruptly*. There is a Richards, you know, in my new book, and this morning I decided to end a chapter on that. *Richards rose abruptly*. So you can see how the confusion arises."

I sighed. "It only remains for me to add that a Rose by any other name—"

"Cecil," interrupted Lucy with unwonted definiteness, "did it." She poked about among the flowers on her left hand for the paper which lay on her right. "I've worked it out."

"My dear Lucy, you really mustn't . . ."

At this moment Basil entered the hall and Lucy caught sight of him. "Basil," she said prosaically and raising her voice, "Cecil did it." She found her piece of paper and began to wave it in the air. Still waving it, she again moved to the bell and rang. "Rose, these had better go in the library too. Why do you think Cecil should say he was praying at half-past seven last night?"

Rose, to whom this emphatic question had every appearance of being directly addressed, gave a startled yelp and set down the bowl abruptly and all but disastrously on the table. We had to stand in great embarrassment until she had recovered sufficiently to take herself off.

"Lucy," said Basil, "if you *could* be a little more collected—"

I nodded severely. "Yes, indeed. The girl appeared scared to an unreasonable degree. So much so, I hope, that she will refrain from gossiping in the servants' hall."

Lucy contrived to look momentarily contrite. "I am so sorry, Basil. But when I have just worked something out—"

"If you will tell us just what you have worked *out* perhaps that will be the safest way of working it *off*."

"*One—*"

"What?"

"*One:* why did Cecil say he was praying at the time of the crime?"

"Perhaps," I suggested, "because he was. Some people do."

"*Two*"—Lucy peered at her paper and turned it sideways— "*Two:* why is he so scared of the doctors?"

"It is possible—"

"Or we may better put it this way: why is he so scared of *medical science?*" And Lucy looked up from her paper as if she had achieved a very cogent formulation indeed. "I will tell you. It is because he is afraid it may detect the lie!"

We looked at her incredulously.

"Something about blood-pressure. I have no doubt that a heart-specialist like Sir Mervyn understands the technique. A little machine. They would tie it on and say 'Did you try to shoot your brother?' And then the machine would ring a bell."

"Lucy," I said, "Anne would say you had bells in the belfry. Or campanophilia. First Shakespeare's bells and now this. It is immoderate."

But Lucy was not to be checked by raillery. She turned to Basil as to a more sympathetic listener. "*Three*." She tapped the table decisively with her scissors. "*Three* is the motive. Who stands to gain most by Wilfred's death? Cecil."

Basil tried to interpose; he took a different line from mine. "Lucy, don't you see any indecency in indulging this fantasy at the expense of your nephews? You are letting your habitual imaginings run away with you." He looked at the chrysanthemums. "Turn your mind to something else."

At this Lucy really did look slightly dashed and I was prompted to intervene. "I suspect, Basil, that Lucy is only in the van. Everybody in the house is beginning to build up one fantasy or another. And most of them at the expense of relations. Appleby pointed out the inevitability of this to me last night. And Cecil—though I don't myself believe Lucy's theory—is as fair game as the rest."

"That reminds me," said Lucy. "I think it very likely that he will take wing. It's very difficult. In the ordinary way I should explain the situation to the police—particularly since there is that pleasant Mr. Appleby. But being a nephew makes it rather different, don't you agree? But then Wilfred is a nephew too. I wish Cecil hadn't done it." She looked quite distressed. "I shall tell him so if I get the chance."

"If you take my advice," said Basil, "you will keep your interesting ideas entirely to yourself. And as for Cecil's taking flight, I think it most unlikely. Actually he was going to-day to lunch with one of his important parents in the city somewhere. But he seems determined to keep to his room. He is there with Cotton now. What will happen when this colleague of Wale's turns up heaven knows."

There was a sound of footsteps on the stairs. Cotton and the attendant Tripet appeared. "A flat roof," Cotton was saying. "Remember that, Tripet; a flat roof. Nothing more natural."

"Yes, sir."

"No agitation, Tripet; no agitation at all. Our business took longer than was expected, no doubt, and Dr. Foxcroft was in a hurry."

"No doubt, sir."

"For an athletic man—a schoolmaster, mark you—the drop would be nothing out of the way. We were not surprised, Tripet. We felt no surprise at all."

"None, sir."

"Our client, though indignant at what appears to have been some indiscretion on the part of his medical adviser, was calm. Eh, Tripet?—calm."

"Calm, sir."

Cotton advanced towards Basil. "Our business is concluded, Sir Basil. I had to advise Dr. Foxcroft that what he proposed was—um—inexpedient. Dr. Foxcroft then went out."

"Went out?"

"Dr. Foxcroft went out by the window. An urgent appointment, I should judge. We last saw him making considerable speed across the park. A charming person. I was very glad to be able to advise him."

And Cotton looked briskly about him for his hat and coat. Lucy Chigwidden, her arms full of chrysanthemums, made an expressive grimace at Basil and myself.

The morning was inevitably restless. Out of sheer need to wander I went up to Hubert's attic. It was likely that he would be working there, and I could present myself as bearer of the intelligence that his sitter had decamped. But Hubert was not in the attic. Once more, it was tenanted by Horace Cudbird.

"The chief news," I said, "is that Cambrell was prowling about this house last night very much as if it were an hotel."

Cudbird appeared to be contemplating his fifty-shilling suit dubiously in the cheval-glass. "Fancy that, now. Those free and easy upper-class ways. A liberty, I should call that. A regular liberty, Mr. Ferryman." He transferred his attention to the concave mirror.

"Do you happen to have seen Basil this morning?"

Cudbird chuckled. "Come now, Mr. Ferryman. The reviewers would call that rather labouring the irony. I just slipped in and up. Mind you, I want to see Hubert Roper." He paused and turned to the big mirror. "To do him a bit of good, of course."

"I'm sure Hubert will be very pleased."

"He might do me a painting of the Priory." Cudbird

looked at me sharply. "It would be nice to have a record."

"A record!" I cried aghast.

He chuckled again at my dismay. "Don't worry. The ruins, you know, are protected. Scheduled, they call it. The Office of Works will come down and put up a little lodge with a couple of turnstiles and a roll of sixpenny tickets. And there will be notices telling folk to keep off the grass." He turned away from the mirror and spoke more soberly. "What news of the wounded man?"

"Wilfred is thought to be out of danger. But as yet they have been unable to question him. Are you still keen on your bet? Perhaps interest will slacken now it's known that murder has not been done."

"Oh, yes. I'm still keen enough." He looked at me shrewdly. "You would like to see interest slacken, as you call it?"

"Yes," I spoke, I believe, with unusual firmness. "At present there is a great deal of useless and extravagant speculation in the family. And even among outsiders as well."

Cudbird shook his head doubtfully. "I don't know that I can be called just an outsider, Mr. Ferryman."

"Surely you cannot pretend that the thing has concerned you?"

"Not if you put it that way—throwing it into the past. But it might concern me—if it went on. Where would my plans be if a second attempt on Sir Basil was successful?"

"It is far from certain that Basil was the intended victim in the first place. Basil himself seems to disbelieve it. And even if it were so I am sure that it was a matter of a crazy impulse that won't recur. I believe Basil is safe."

Cudbird took a couple of paces backwards and eyed me critically. "Well then, say it was Wilfred Foxcroft who was to be shot. Would that make Sir Basil quite safe?"

I stared at him. "But of course it would!"

"Say somebody had a strong and evident motive for killing Foxcroft—and failed in the attempt. Mightn't that person find safety in confusing the issue by taking a subsequent shot at Sir Basil?"

"I hardly think—"

"Or take another line. Say it was Sir Basil himself who tried to shoot Wilfred Foxcroft—and that the police might hit upon a very clear motive for that. Mightn't Sir Basil confuse the issue by taking another shot—not fatal, you know—at himself?"

I felt suddenly out of patience. "My dear sir, it was to escape from very similar ingenuities by a fanciful lady downstairs that I retreated up here. Such notions cannot be useful and may be mischievous. Mrs. Chigwidden has evolved just such a case against Cecil Foxcroft. And, if she has been putting it about, that may very well account for his nervous collapse and bolt."

Cudbird was really surprised. "His bolt—you say Dr. Foxcroft has bolted? Now, that doesn't fit in at all." He looked round the attic as if it had suddenly presented him with a fresh puzzle.

"I really don't believe you can tell whether it fits in or not. The whole framework of the affair is utterly obscure and likely to remain so. And as for your case against Basil, I can only say that you appear to share it with that young puppy Geoffrey. If that is a recommendation, I leave you to judge."

"Geoffrey Roper thinks his uncle shot at Wilfred Fox-croft?"

"Yes. And if you want yet another suspicion I believe Appleby is inclined to suppose that it was Cambrell trying to shoot Basil."

"Wrong, Mr. Ferryman—every one of them. Believe me. And I hold no brief against Sir Basil. It was Sir Basil who was thought to be shot at, all right. Shall I tell you who did the shooting?"

There was a sudden confidence about Cudbird that appalled me despite myself. Once more he had that compelling quality which had constrained us all in the matter of Jim Meech and the canaries. I looked at him helplessly, even with a certain unreasonable anxiety. "Yes," I said. "Tell me who tried to shoot Basil."

Cudbird's eye swept round the studio. "It's as clear as—" He broke off and frowned. "Or rather that's just what it's not. It's *there*, all right. But it's difficult to get straight. It's as distorted"—he paused and considered—"as my nose in that glass." And he pointed to the concave mirror on the wall.

CHAPTER XIX

I WAS peering at the mirror—as if that were at all likely to afford a clue to Cudbird's speculations—when the door opened and Hubert Roper came in. He seemed to have no disposition to question our presence, but walked directly to the window and looked out over the park. I moved to his side. Unbroken snow was below us; beyond, the city sullenly resisted the pressure of a leaden sky. To the left, and closer than I had ever realised them to be, back-to-back houses spilt themselves down the valley-side in parallel rows, like grimy tentacles abruptly lopped. Everywhere, above black roofs snow-powdered, slow smoke rose grey and black to heaven, so that the city showed like a vast and cinereous altar whose useless offerings smouldered in a void. A lurid sun hung low as a furnace door in a foundry, or like a burning football tumbled between the goal-posts of the brewery chimneys. And far away down the valley, as if to suggest that here was but an outer circle in the inferno of industrialism, lay a blacker smudge that told of iron and steel in a neighbour town. That somewhere winter brought the earth repose, that somewhere the freshets drew their speed from unsullied snow: this was impossible to believe. Hubert looked intently at the brick and slate and smoke. "My God," he said, "what a fool I was to go south and paint their damned silly mugs!" He turned to Cudbird. "Do you know that I've given twenty years to painting mugs that are all as alike as the bottoms of identical twins? While all the time there was that." And he jerked his thumb backwards at the window.

I was startled; for me the scene spelt nothing but depression. But Cudbird appeared to be startled too. "You find faces monotonous? Now, that's very interesting. I should hardly have believed it. Why, even canaries—"

Hubert shook his head absently. "My dear man, canaries live in a state of nature—more or less. But human features are coming to compress themselves more and more within a few masks. Three or four masks to each sex in each social class, and faces have to conform. It is very boring, believe me. Of course back-to-backs are monotonous too. But one can put a quarter of a mile of atmosphere between oneself and them. And they gain in mystery and beauty with every yard."

"A case," I said, "of distance lending enchantment to the view."

It was a banal remark, and Hubert contrived to give the impression of inspecting it gloomily. "Distance," he remarked presently, "would lend some enchantment to those confounded policemen. They're here again, you know. First Leader badgering people about times and places. And now Appleby collecting slips of ivy in the garden. You may well look surprised. I came on him while he was at it and asked him if it was by way of souvenir. He said that was it. Incidentally, he was looking at the stuff in all gloom, as if it had let him down. I hope he grows really discouraged and goes away."

"You don't think," Cudbird asked, "that the shooting had better be cleared up?"

Hubert made no reply but perched himself on the table amid a litter of sketches. He picked up a crayon and began to scrawl on the back of a portfolio, his gaze moodily lost in the cheval-glass. I broke the silence. "Perhaps you agree with me that the thing was a momentary madness and is best forgotten?"

Hubert glanced at me vaguely. "Momentary? Oh, assuredly. Takes no time to pull a trigger."

I was disturbed by this deliberate inconsequence. "Well, perhaps not quite as momentary as that. Appleby has a theory that someone saw a chance of shooting Basil, went to get a weapon, and failed to notice that in the meantime Wilfred had taken Basil's place. That gives the thing a certain sinister deliberation. But even if that happened I regard the whole series of events as a single aberration. And if I know anything of human nature—our sort of human nature in this house—the only sequel will be horror and recoil. There will be no second attempt. Don't you agree, Hubert?"

Hubert stopped fiddling with his crayon. "I can't say I do. No. I think your position is forced and risky. Decidedly risky. The truth is, Arthur, that you are the sort of person who would do a good deal to avoid a vulgar scandal. Cudbird, don't you read him that way?"

Cudbird said nothing. Hubert looked at Cudbird as if detachedly interested in the way that Cudbird was looking at him. In the silence there floated in through the window a sound of sparrows scuffling in the eaves. I felt baffled and alarmed. "Appleby—" I began.

"It's odd," interrupted Hubert, "how this Appleby stuffs Arthur with ideas and sends him running round.

The police are telling us a lot. But what ought we to tell the police?" His fingers jerked nervously on the crayon. "Where we were at the time—that sort of thing. I've told them I was in my room." He laughed vaguely. "Except for yourself, Arthur, about everybody has told them so. I wonder how many fibs that involves?"

Cudbird, who had picked up a drawing and perched it critically against the wall, turned round on this. "Perhaps everyone concerned has an irrelevant secret to hide. But somewhere someone has a secret which is *relevant*. It's teasing, you know." He glanced at his watch. "Twelve hours now, and the cat is still in the bag. Will it turn restless and give itself away? Or all the time"—and Cudbird set up another drawing and cocked a considering head at it—"is there some chink through which a whisker or the tip of a tail is showing?" He nodded his head in the slightly oracular way he occasionally affected. "There's a relevant secret somewhere."

"Are you sure?"

We turned round at the sound of a new voice. It was Appleby who had slipped into the room. Viewed by daylight he looked older than I remembered him. Or it may have been a certain air of anxiety which gave this effect: he had the appearance of a man dissatisfied with his own efforts.

"Are you sure?" he repeated. "What if the cat is a Manx cat, with no tail to protrude? And that's how I really feel about this problem: something missing."

"A Manx cat?" said Hubert. "Ferryman here would like to see the mystery behave like the Cheshire sort and just fade away."

Appleby looked soberly from one to the other of us. "Something missing," he reiterated. "That's it."

As if he were being fitted with one of his new shiny suits, Cudbird placed himself carefully between the big mirror and the cheval-glass. "Well," he said, "Cecil Foxcroft is said to be missing. What about that? But I'm not sure myself that we haven't everything to hand for solving the riddle."

Appleby paced across the attic, turned round, surveyed first Hubert and then myself. I had the uncomfortable impression that he was recording us as thoroughly unsatisfactory exhibits. "No," he said—and his manner was brusque as it had not hitherto been. "There's something missing, and I know it."

Hubert swung himself off the table. "Rather a negative piece of knowledge, is it not?" He took up a palette and began to scrape at it. "And we should hate to think of you wasting your time."

If this was a hint Appleby ignored it. "I really don't think I'm doing that," he said. "This conviction that something is missing—it may be useful. Yes"—his voice was hesitating in evident absence of mind—"yes . . . I think you may find it that. It is what I felt from the first. Otherwise I would scarcely have pushed in."

We looked at him in perplexity. "Mr. Appleby believes," I said, "that the missing piece will fall into place as soon as he remembers a bit of poetry—something about mist and snow."

Turning away from the window through which he had been peering at the back-to-backs, Appleby shook his head. "It's not exactly a matter of a missing *piece*.

Nor—however interesting Dr. Foxcroft's proceedings may be—of a missing man." He smiled suddenly. "If *I* had this fellow Beevor after me I'd nip out of a window myself. Incidentally, Beevor has arrived. He and Wale are discussing the case *in absentia* in the library. Not, one would imagine, the most satisfactory of clinical methods. And Mrs. Chigwidden has been in conference with them too. She has a theory." Appleby was speaking in disjointed sentences which made me suspect that his mind was not entirely on what he said. "Perhaps Dr. Foxcroft has a theory also." He glanced at us ironically. "Who hasn't?"

"I understood," I said, "that Lucy Chigwidden was reluctant to divulge her theory to the police."

"She is quite unaware that she has divulged it." And Appleby treated me to a grin which might have been reckoned—unfairly perhaps—faintly conceited. "Or that it is wholly untenable." He turned to Hubert. "For there is one—just one—piece of positive knowledge that I do possess. Dr. Foxcroft didn't fire that shot. But anyone else—barring Wilfred Foxcroft himself—might have. Any of you might have." Appleby paused and I had the impression that all this was somehow a deliberate marking time. "Dr. Foxcroft alone has an alibi."

"Cecil has an alibi!" I cried in astonishment. "But we understood—"

"Yes. But Dr. Foxcroft's devotions were not performed in solitude. In fact"—and for a moment Appleby looked the most wooden of policeman—"the young person's name is Rose. The servants have been questioned; the fact emerged."

"This," I said, "is what one gets by raking about. And no wonder that Rose was upset by Lucy's remarks. I am shocked, and I can see that Cudbird is too."

Hubert chuckled without much mirth. "One imagines that Cecil's advances would be indecisive and embarrassed. I do not suppose that Rose lost her virtue—or as much as her breath."

"But Cecil has certainly lost his head." I turned to Appleby. "Is this indiscretion known to Wale? And is that why . . ."

Appleby had gone to the window and was drumming gently on the sill; it struck me again that he was waiting for something other than the conversation of Hubert, Cudbird and myself. Now he turned round. "It would hardly explain his wanting to make a will. Nor his sudden bolt."

"He was due," said Hubert, "to lunch with a parent— awful man called Podman who makes motor-bodies over in Riverton. I suppose someone ought to ring up and say he's ill. For I suppose he *is* ill. Going to be dam' well dammed up by Beevor." Over this joke—characteristic of Geoffrey rather than of his father—Hubert laughed with even less enjoyment than before. He tossed his palette on the table and paced restlessly across the attic. "What the devil of a lot of interesting talk. Nothing bores me more. Can't we have a spot of action?"

"Action?" said Appleby. He smiled with an affectation of vague geniality. "Oh, no. We just wait about." He put his hands in his pockets.

Cudbird, as if prompted to take up a contrary attitude, moved briskly towards the door. "To keep up with

John's waiting about," he said, "you have to look pretty
nippy. As for action—"

"Yes, action." Hubert's voice rose insistently. "This
chatter gets nowhere." He paused, and I was conscious
of his giving me an odd look. "If only the unknown
would take another crack at Basil the thing might begin
to work out."

"I think," said Cudbird, "that Sir Basil is safe enough
at the moment."

"From what you said last night"—I turned to Appleby
—"I gather you really think there might be some danger
of Basil's being attacked? And Cudbird has several notions which point to the same possibility."

Appleby shook his head; he seemed increasingly pre-
occupied. "No, I hardly think there's much danger. Perhaps I was just trying something out on Sir Basil." He
smiled his absent and engaging smile. "As Mr. Roper
says: a lot of interesting talk. All over the house. Theories
rather than deeds, perhaps, are incubating at Belrive.
Don't you think so, Mr. Cudbird?"

Cudbird was still standing by the door; his reply was
lost in the sudden screech of the Cambrell siren. "Twelve
o'clock," I said, "and it seems as if we had scarcely finished breakfast."

"Twelve o'clock?" Appleby took his hands out of his
pockets and looked innocently surprised. "Dear me, perhaps we ought to be going downstairs."

"Perhaps you ought," said Hubert. "You have all been
very generous of your time already. And I mustn't be
greedy and expect more than my share."

Appleby amiably smiled. "I am sure—and Mr. Cudbird

is even more sure—that you are quite absorbed in your work." He glanced at the brewer and I thought that his smile took on the character of a private joke. "But perhaps you will come down too? I have just remembered" —and Appleby's features took on the expression of a man who had just remembered—"that Leader is proposing a sort of conference at twelve."

"A conference?" I asked suspiciously.

"In the library. We must hurry or we shall be late."

With Cudbird leading the way we trooped downstairs. Everybody was in the library—or everybody except Basil and Cecil. Even Cambrell had appeared once more. And at a desk near the middle of the room sat Leader supported by a sergeant of police. We edged ourselves into chairs, and I noticed that Appleby disappeared unobtrusively into a shadowy corner. Then we waited. Nobody had anything to say, or any apparent idea of what was going forward. The effect was uncommonly solemn.

A long and somewhat fidgety silence was broken by an important cough from Leader. "Our business—" he began.

The sergeant murmured something in his ear. Leader broke off and nodded. The sergeant rose and rang a bell. A constable appeared, was given whispered instructions, and departed. The police, we had to realise, had descended upon Belrive in a flood.

"I am afraid," said Leader, "that we can scarcely begin without Sir Basil." He tapped the desk impatiently. "But he is unlikely to be long. He promised to be here with the rest of you at noon." And Leader fell to studying his notebook. It had the appearance of having grown larger overnight. He turned a page; the rustle fell upon an increasingly nervous silence.

A couple of minutes went by. Leader, I thought, was passing from mere impatience to apprehensiveness. At the sound of a footstep in the hall every eye turned towards the door: it was the constable again. He murmured to Leader, crossed the room and murmured to Appleby. And it seemed to me that between the two men there passed a guarded but startled glance.

Silence descended once more; once more it was broken by the sound of footsteps. But this time of running footsteps. The door flew open: Richards appeared with yet another constable behind him. He looked distractedly round the room, hurried across to Leader. "Sir Basil," he cried; "Sir Basil has been attacked in the ruins. An attempt to murder him. They're bringing him up to the house."

CHAPTER XX

FAR ADVANCED as I am into the territory of Lucy Chigwidden, I see I have yielded in the matter of chapterisation to just Lucy's sense of effect. Richards' announcement makes a capital little curtain—a curtain which rings
up again immediately on much hubbub and confusion
in the library. But I can at least refrain from exploiting
this. Briefly, what followed was rather like a scene in an
overcrowded classical tragedy. The messenger dashes in
with news of disaster, the chorus makes a great to-do, and
then a second messenger—somewhat less out of breath—
arrives and gives a fuller account of the trouble on hand.
In our case the second messenger was a uniformed inspector of police: I found myself hoping for a moment
that he was that Haines of whose services Appleby had
adroitly deprived us the evening before. His actual name
—if I ever knew it—has long escaped me. I remember
him only as a voice. As that and as a further intimidating
intimation of the manner in which the constabulary were
crowding in upon our mystery.

Wale—once more called upon for emergency services
—hurried from the room. And then the voice struck up.
It appeared that the whole park and gardens were being
patrolled and that the success of this new attack had in
consequence upset the police very much: our second inspector seemed concerned to exculpate his subordinates
to the company at large. He had made an appointment

with Basil, it appeared, to examine the little armoury at the range. He arrived to find Basil unconscious in the ruins.

"A cleverly contrived accident," said the inspector—nominally to Leader, but actually in an indefinably threatening way to the assembled party. "Severely wounded in the head, and beside him a large stone apparently dislodged from the tower. He can't as much as have cried out, poor gentleman, or one of our men would have heard. A devilish trick enough."

The Voice was clearly of a more emotional habit than those of his colleagues whom we had encountered hitherto. He shook his head in a thoroughly gloomy way and had to be prompted by Appleby, speaking from his corner.

"Any signs in the snow? Anyone reported as having been seen about the park?"

The Voice shook its head. "Not a sign. And not a soul. And of the present company—Dr. Foxcroft excepted—everyone seems pretty well accounted for."

I felt someone stir suddenly beside me: it was Geoffrey Roper. He leant forward as if to interrupt and then, thinking better of it, sank back in his chair.

"There's one queer thing, though. Sir Basil's waistcoat and shirt were unbuttoned. Looks as if the person responsible had tried to make sure he was done for."

I noticed Appleby looking momentarily disconcerted, and I wondered if some theory of his was upset by this intelligence. But for that matter we were all undoubtedly very much upset. This fresh disaster, coming on top of the original shooting and Cecil's madness, had got us pretty well on the run.

Lucy was the first person to venture a contribution to the deliberations of the police. "Perhaps," she said nervously, "it really *was* an accident. Looking up at the tower I have often thought that it was in dangerous disrepair. Perhaps a stone really fell off and hurt Basil." Her eye became abstracted, as it did when she was consulting some world of inner experience. "After all, the most extraordinary coincidences do happen."

The answer to this suggestion came from Wale, who had reappeared at the door. "Casually falling masonry," he said, "doesn't behave with surgical skill." He crossed the room and sat down somewhat wearily in his former place. "The blow could not have been more deftly delivered."

There was silence. We were all faintly bewildered without for a moment knowing why. Then Hubert Roper spoke. "But surely it wasn't a very efficient attack—supposing it to be that? Basil, we gather, is still alive—even if the wound is severe?"

"Severe?" Wale snorted contemptuously. "It might look severe to an innocent eye. But I assure you that Roper was no more than stunned—and uncommonly neatly too. There was never the slightest danger. He will have nothing but a bit of a headache twenty-four hours from now."

From the far end of the room came the clear voice of Anne Grainger. "But the police *will* think us an ineffective lot. First Wilfred messily and inconclusively shot and now this. I call it humiliating, positively. But I suppose"—and she looked collectedly round at our disapproving stares—"that it's pretty typical of our decaying social class. Nothing done quite right."

Leader frowned. The Voice frowned a great deal more menacingly than Leader. And if Appleby, on the contrary, seemed pleased we drew small comfort from that. We were thoroughly discomfited. It might have appeared impossible that these appalling pleasantries of Anne's could be capped. But capped they were—and needless to say by Geoffrey.

"I'm sorry about Basil's headache," Geoffrey said. "It will be such a horridly uncomfortable thing to take to quod."

I recall Appleby leaning back in his chair—and as I do so the image of a rising curtain again presents itself to me. For him the play was beginning. And, though largely passive, he was more than a simple spectator. There was something about him of the manner in which the producer finally takes his place in the stalls. And I thought he was particularly satisfied when Geoffrey suddenly rose excitedly and pointed at him—pointed with a gesture that held much more of drama than decent manners.

"Look at him," said Geoffrey. "And look at the others." His hand swept round Leader, the second inspector, the sergeant, the waiting constable. "Do you think they believe this stuff about someone having attacked Basil? Of course not. And any more foolery is a waste of time."

Hubert Roper had been watching his son's extravagant conduct with a vaguely disapproving eye. But now he nodded. "Intolerable waste of time, all right. Still, one doesn't feel you're likely to brisken things up by shouting, my boy." And Hubert, having exerted himself to the extent of this unusual rebuke, sat back and evidently debated with himself the propriety of lighting a cigarette.

"Let Basil," continued Geoffrey unperturbed, "be removed in a big black van. Then we can get on. I don't mean I don't think it a pity. I do. There was some sense in that notion of a meteorological station. And as for the selling-up I for one should not object—and Belrive, after all, would be mine one day. If a person like Wilfred, who has no notions at all except of just mucking comfortably along, announces he is going to get in the way of an idea —well, I think it quite sound to see that he gets in the way of a bullet. But Basil shouldn't have muffed it. Shows he must be losing grasp. Makes one rather feel he might muff the antarctic business too. And then we should have lost Belrive for nothing. I'm sorry for Basil. But he took a risk and now the sooner he takes that van the less fuss there will be. For you may be sure that these smart alecks"—and Geoffrey waved a finger at Leader and his sergeant—"won't let anybody off. Jugging chaps is all their joy."

I had listened in stupefaction to this long speech, and I suppose the rest of us had done the same. It was Appleby who was the first to speak. "So you think, Mr. Roper, that Sir Basil shot Mr. Foxcroft because Mr. Foxcroft might interfere with Sir Basil's projected expedition?"

"That's what *you* think, Mr. Appleby. I'm just helping you to the complete motive. It's bound to come out and may as well come out quickly. Of course they had quarrelled long ago while climbing a mountain. I don't know why: perhaps even in those days Wilfred needed a spot too much comfort. There may have been a half-conscious carry-over from that to the present affair. But I don't think so. Basil's decision to eliminate Wilfred goes back no further than tea-time yesterday."

Lucy Chigwidden gave a startled exclamation.

"Lucy remembers at least. We were chattering about the sale of Belrive—it was over the muffins when one cackles like anything—and Wilfred said he didn't believe it, but if it were true he knew who could stop Basil. Obviously he meant himself: he's the business man of the family, remember, who would be up in that sort of thing. And just at that moment Basil came in. He'd plainly heard and we all felt pretty fools. I remember Cecil began yattering about his *Serious Call*. But it was poor old Wilfred's serious call, and pretty nearly his last. Basil, I say, who is a remote and ruthless bird really, wasn't going to stand for having his expedition wrecked. He took a shot at Wilfred. And of course nobody attacked him in the ruins this morning. He simply felt these worthies"—the finger pointed at Appleby and the Voice this time—"were probably after him and he decided to cloud the issue by arranging a bogus assault."

Less than an hour before, I remembered, Cudbird had been putting just this possibility to me. I stared at Geoffrey, horrified by the brusque and almost careless conviction with which he spoke. It was impossible to resist the conviction that he believed what he said; believed not only in the facts as he had related them but in the morality behind them as well. Basil had possessed a notion, and was entitled to eliminate Wilfred, who had no notion, if Wilfred interfered. But Basil had muffed it, and the sooner he went off to prison the sooner we could get back to our desks and studios. Hence a sudden zeal for the despatch of justice. I can only say that the perversity of this willingness to throw an uncle to the bloodhounds left me gasping. When I had a little recovered it was to hear with considerable relief the colourless voice of Leader.

"And you would say, sir, that a bogus assault can be staged in that way?" Leader paused with heavy irony. "That a man can successfully stun himself on the back of the head: your experience bears out the possibility of that?"

It was only momentarily that Geoffrey looked uncertain. "If one were Basil—yes. He's no end of an athlete and a clever chap. A climber too, with joints like a contortionist. And quite abnormal resolution. Yes, Basil could do it all right."

"You say"—Appleby spoke for the first time—"that Sir Basil is an athlete. Would you also say that he is a good shot?"

Geoffrey grinned. "Very good, indeed."

"In fact, about as good as you yourself are bad?"

Geoffrey's grin broadened; he plainly felt that he had something up his sleeve. "Just about that."

"Then how do you account for the fact that at what can have been no more than a few paces Sir Basil failed to kill his man? The bullet as we know, got the right lung. Do you suggest that this remote and ruthless person—as you describe your uncle—was so agitated that he was unable to take proper aim? Or why was Mr. Fox-croft so imperfectly shot?"

The last phrase made me start: it had been used by Anne or by Geoffrey himself when Appleby and I were spying on them in the ruins. And I remembered, too, something that Appleby had said of them immediately after: he had spoken of them as having penetrated to the heart of the mystery. And just as I recollected this Geoffrey spoke again. "Yes," he said, "why was Wilfred so imperfectly shot? The core of the thing is in that."

It was a queer scene. Geoffrey was still standing up in the middle of the library—slightly flushed, perhaps slightly nervous, like a child put up to recite. And scattered about the room was the quite sizeable auditory of family and police. The purpose for which we had been brought together before the attack on Basil seemed vanished or in abeyance; in his extremely ill-considered attempt to expedite the winding-up of the mystery Geoffrey was being given his head. And he went into a full gallop now.

"Basil has changed early. He has been working in his study. He comes out and finds Wilfred emerging from the library here, unable to write a letter because Lucy has made away with all the note paper. Basil sees his chance, he tells Wilfred to go into the study and write the letter at his desk. Then he gets a gun."

Leader had applied himself to his notebook. Some of us cast uneasy glances at each other about the room. There was something peculiarly macabre in Geoffrey's brisk statement that then his uncle got a gun.

"What is the position? Wilfred, sitting down to write his letter, will be facing the window. Basil will have left the curtains a foot or two apart: it is his habit. Now one of two things may happen. Wilfred, who doesn't much care for the cold, may draw them to before he sits down. In that case Basil has only to step through the window, part them an inch or so and fire. But suppose Wilfred happens to have left the curtains undisturbed? Then there is a difficulty. Arthur, you went poking round with these people last night. If Wilfred was sitting at the desk with the curtains a foot or two apart just what could he see?"

The question was suddenly pitched at me and I hesitated. Not unnaturally. I was wholly indisposed to assist this wanton attempt to convict Basil of the shooting. But Appleby's eye turned to me in mild inquiry and I felt bound to reply. For a moment, however, I fenced. "What do you mean: just what could he see?"

"What could he see of someone on the terrace—standing out there, moving about, approaching the window?"

"If someone were walking up and down near the balustrade he would see no more than an uncertain figure taking a stroll."

"Unidentifiable?"

"I think so. In a dinner-jacket, certainly. But if the person faced the house and approached the window—"

"Exactly!" Geoffrey swept a triumphant glance round the company. "Common prudence would dictate that Basil should fire without revealing his identity to Wilfred. However good the shot, Wilfred might be able to gasp out the truth if help came quickly. Basil therefore could stroll up and down by the balustrade. He could stand by the balustrade looking over the garden. Under these conditions he would be no more to Wilfred than an unknown member of the household taking the air before dinner. *Basil could not safely turn round and approach the window.*"

The library was suddenly very still; fidgeting noises had ceased; the only sound was the click of a coal in the grate.

"So consider," said Geoffrey, "just what was going on at the range yesterday morning. Just what sort of trick-shooting." He wheeled abruptly round. "Cambrell, are you wearing that watch now?"

This was sensation. I felt a cold trickle of horror travel down my spine. And Cambrell jumped much as if he himself were being accused. Then he nodded, fumbled at his left wrist and laid something on a table before him. It was a watch on a bright metal bracelet.

Geoffrey continued what had become his speech for the prosecution. "I was interested in the trick—the trick of shooting backwards that we heard of afterwards—and I managed to make out how it was done. Cambrell faced away from the target, tucked the barrel of his revolver under his left arm, and took his pipe from his mouth with his left hand. That was the key. The left wrist goes up, the cuff slips down and—if the light is right—the polished bracelet serves as a little mirror. With practice one can no doubt make a very fair shot."

Horror grew upon me. I remembered the words with which I had myself heard Basil greet Cambrell's trick: "A gunman's trick: I think I could do it myself." Giving way to an irresistible impulse, I cried out: "It's non-sense; it can't be true!"

Curious glances were directed on me only for a moment: then everyone turned back to Geoffrey as I sank back in my chair. Whatever was to be thought of the plausibility of his story he had his auditory gripped.

"So there you are. Basil stands by the balustrade, as if watching the garden or Cudbird's beastly bottle. Then he takes a few paces backwards—it is a natural action if one is getting a view—and plays Cambrell's trick on Wilfred. But he isn't quite up to it and he muffs"—Geoffrey paused slightly and looked round him almost defiantly --"he muffs the killing."

For perhaps twenty seconds there was silence. Then a voice spoke quietly from the door. "An interesting theory indeed."

We all turned round. It was Basil himself.

CHAPTER XXI

"But it breaks down at the start."

Basil was very pale and had a light bandage round his head; he advanced somewhat unsteadily as he spoke and lowered himself cautiously into a chair. Wale had risen hastily; this appearance was evidently against orders. But Basil peremptorily waved him back.

"I shall be right enough. And I agree with Geoffrey in one thing: that this affair had better be cleared up at once—however painful that clear-up may be. And the first thing to establish is that Geoffrey's case breaks down at the start. The motive does not exist."

Appleby had settled back in his chair with the appearance of a man who expects that matters will now work themselves smoothly out. Leader was applying himself steadily to his notebook, for all the world as if he were reporting the most humdrum of political meetings. The Voice was looking at us each in turn with evident and deepening disapproval. My own eye was all for Basil. He was indeed a person somewhat cold and remote; that he might—as Geoffrey averred—be ruthless on occasion I was not at all disposed to doubt. I awaited what he had to say with a good deal of nervousness. And this was increased when I realised that beneath his calm Basil was angry—angry as I had never known him before.

"The suggestion is that I shot Wilfred because I overheard him declare that he knew who could prevent my selling Belrive. But if Geoffrey were at all a man of affairs he would realise what nonsense that is. I am proposing to organise a scientific expedition to the financing of which I am at present giving virtually my whole time and thoughts. I have gone some way towards negotiating a sale of this property. Is it likely that I am incompetent to discover any possible legal impediment that there may be? Is it conceivable that at this stage Wilfred should be able to step in, waving some forgotten deed or paper, and stop the whole thing? Such an idea could only be evolved by a person"—Basil paused and seemed to turn a shade paler—"by a person under the strongest promptings to evolve . . . something."

It was at this point, I think, that most of us grasped the unpleasant truth that Basil was concerned with rather more than exculpating himself. I saw Horace Cudbird stir warily in his chair and look speculatively at Cambrell; I saw Lucy shiver and Mervyn Wale lean forward to throw a log on the fire. Then Basil's level voice claimed all my attention again.

"It is true that I heard what Wilfred said at tea. I went back to my study and thought about it. Wilfred is a person with a great deal to say for himself—the sort of person, in fact, to whom one does not always greatly attend. Nevertheless he holds a position of responsibility and has not the habit of talking at random in matters of this sort. What he had said was virtually this: that he himself could prevent my going forward with my particular plan for disposing of this estate. After careful thought I found that I could attach only one significance to such a statement. It surprised me."

Basil made a long pause—less for effect, I imagine, than because the effort of talking was considerable. "In the present temper of this household other explanations are possible. I can see a certain type of mind"—and Basil's eye went fleetingly to his sister—"which might suppose that Wilfred was proposing to come at me with a gun. No doubt that would do the trick. But the actual explanation was less sensational. I say it surprised me. For Wilfred's attitude to Belrive has always been somewhat off-hand; he has adopted the appearance of thinking the place an anachronism—an encumbrance on potentially valuable industrial land. For this reason—and perhaps because there was a residual coolness between us—I had held no direct communication with him on my plans. But now it was perfectly clear to me that in this I had been acting wrongly. It was perfectly clear that Wilfred, who is a very wealthy man, was prepared to buy Belrive himself. I took the opportunity of speaking to him, therefore, before going upstairs to change. It was as I thought. He said simply that he was interested in the project of a meteorological station and would buy Belrive at the highest figure I had so far been offered. And just as I preferred Cudbird's proposal to Cambrell's so I prefer Wilfred's to Cudbird's. And I know that you, Cudbird, will not suggest that anything had been concluded between us."

Cudbird made what appeared to be a cordial affirmative reply. It was drowned however by the crisp voice of Anne. "Then I suppose it was Mr. Cudbird who shot Wilfred. Geoffrey, why didn't we think of that?"

"Yes," pursued Anne; "that is it." She turned a bright smile and a hard eye upon the Voice—having divined in him, no doubt, the most readily outraged person in the room. "How very *clear*. Mr. Cudbird hears what Wilfred proposes to do, so he walks in at the window and shoots him. The situation is then as it was, and Mr. Cudbird bottles Belrive. Belrive Beers are Best. Try our Priory Entire." She turned to Cudbird. "You do see," she asked with innocent earnestness, "how my explanation has the grand virtue of *simplicity?*"

Cudbird contemplated her impassively. "Perhaps, Miss Anne, you will tell us how Sir Basil came to be attacked just now in the ruins. Maybe I have just formed the habit of guns and bludgeons?"

Anne shook her head. "That I leave to the police." Again she turned her smile on the Voice. "It would be nice that they should be left *some* explaining to do. Don't they remind you of a row of powerful locomotive engines laid up in a yard? I can see the beginnings of a film of rust over Mr. Appleby already. Inspector Leader is quite a Pacific type. And on this gentleman here"—and Anne bowed gravely to the Voice—"one feels it is only necessary to pull a piece of string to get the most magnificent hoot."

The constable sniggered; the Voice breathed hard—thus unwittingly giving point to Anne's comparison; the rest of us attempted to maintain what is called a frozen silence. Presently Leader spoke. "Miss Grainger's suggestion," he said, "will be considered in its place. If it *has* a place, that is to say." He paused as if calling our attention to this repartee. "And now, Sir Basil, there is a most important point. Mr. Foxcroft, as you know, is unable to answer questions, and one can't tell what turn his condition may take. So we want some sort of independent testimony to this resolution of his to buy Belrive. You will realise—"

"Quite so." Basil was impatient and I could tell from this that he was angrier than before—Anne's conduct being no doubt the cause. "There is, I believe, something like evidence. Wilfred remarked that it was a big thing and he would have down his solicitor. And he scribbled out a telegram for Richards to send off there and then. It specifically mentioned the conveyancing of the estate."

"Thank you. That is most satisfactory."

Appleby stirred in his chair as if he did not think it satisfactory at all. It seemed to be his policy that the locomotives should remain as long as possible idling in their yard. "Sir Basil," he said, "has something further to tell us—or so I imagine."

"I have." Basil squared himself in his chair. "And I begin with what has been called the core of the thing. In Geoffrey's phrase: why was Wilfred so imperfectly shot? We have had one explanation: Wilfred was only badly wounded because a difficult piece of trick-shooting was involved. But we have seen that for this there is no basis whatever."

Leader raised his eyes from his notebook. "Hardly that, Sir Basil. We have seen that a particular motive for your shooting Mr. Foxcroft will not hold. But the trick-shooting remains on the carpet just the same. And I must say it seems not a bad explanation of a very puzzling feature of the case. Logic, sir—we must stick to logic."

It could not be denied that Basil's logic had gone momentarily off the rails; he acknowledged this himself with a nod which must have caused him a good deal of physical discomfort. "Very well. I merely offer you, then, a simpler explanation of why Wilfred was not killed. *Killing Wilfred was not the intention of the person who fired the shot.*"

"You mean that the shot was meant for yourself?" Leader's pencil suspended itself in air. Very faintly, Appleby sighed.

"I mean"—Basil's voice was perfectly patient again—"that the person who fired the shot at Wilfred didn't mean to *kill* Wilfred. Or not outright." Basil paused and appeared to take a long breath. "Geoffrey, is that not so?"

On me at least the words had the effect of physical impact. That Geoffrey should hurl a reckless accusation at his uncle was not out of keeping with much in his character. But that Basil should promptly retort the charge upon his nephew appeared for a moment unbelievably horrible. And for the second time in this fantastic conference I was prompted to attempt intervention. "Basil," I cried, "stop, in heaven's name! It isn't so. Haven't we had mad talk enough?"

I found that in my excitement I had jumped to my feet. Now I sat down trembling. I was aware of Appleby's eye upon me—an oddly approving eye considering the incoherence of what I had said. And once more I was powerfully aware that of everything that was going on in the library this quiet young man was indefinably in control. The others, too, I think, were becoming aware of this; it was to Appleby and not to Leader that Basil was clearly addressing himself.

"We have had mad talk only as a consequence of mad action—action so mad that I should be failing in my duty if I did not expose it. Geoffrey is guilty of the attack on Wilfred. And his motive was mere avarice."

Geoffrey, who had not spoken since his own theory of the crime had been exploded, said nothing now. But he laughed. In the circumstances it was a curiously inoffensive laugh, brief and unforced.

But Basil paid no attention. "Geoffrey and Anne have been mad to get something out of Wilfred; they seem to consider it a right. And Wilfred has been putting Anne off—injudiciously, I think it must be said. And I believe there has been another cause of friction—probably of passion—which I shall not mention in this rather large gathering."

Basil put a weary hand to his bandaged head. The possible emotional tangle between Wilfred, his ward and Geoffrey was certainly not a thing to air. But it was the only basis that I could see for building up any sort of case. It occurred to me that Wale would have done well to insist on getting Basil away. This turning upon Geoffrey was wholly unlike him, and the clearest evidence that his judgment was clouded by the attack he had suffered. But plainly he had to go forward now with what he had to say.

"Geoffrey's action has turned upon an odd calculation as to Wilfred's behaviour in certain circumstances. Wilfred had settled nothing upon Anne. He had bequeathed her nothing. But he had every intention of doing so, and his delay proceeded, it would appear, simply from a foolish desire to preserve a sense of power. But if put in mortal danger—dying or believing he was about to die—Wilfred would do what he conceived to be the right thing." Basil smiled grimly. "And what Geoffrey and Anne believed to be the right thing. And that is why Geoffrey didn't shoot to kill outright."

Basil sank back in his chair amid a dead silence, and once more Wale got up and moved across the room towards him. And then Basil spoke again. "Arthur can witness to the moment at which the plan was put in Geoffrey's head—unwittingly, I hope and believe—by Anne. It was when—"

Basil's voice tailed off, exhausted. Everybody looked in my direction. I hesitated, though there had come to me a sudden realisation of what was meant. Then I decided that Basil's case, such as it was, had better out. "Yesterday morning during the revolver-practice," I said, "Geoffrey and Anne were talking—resentfully, I fear—about Wilfred's attitude. Basil must have come up in time to hear the end of it." I hesitated in an effort to remember accurately. "What Anne finally said was this: '*Wilfred is going to gather his dependents round the death-bed. And then how infinitely charitable he will be.*'"

Leader's pencil snapped at the point. Anne's wretched witticism could not have been brought out more effectively, I suppose, than thus at the tail of Basil's accusation. And the whole company turned to look at her now.

She was sitting beside Geoffrey and she had put her hand on his. "Geoffrey put out his story," she said steadily, "because he is impulsive and a bit of a blackguard. But Basil can have put out his only because that crack has sent him a bit off his head. He knows much better. Arthur, isn't that so?"

"Basil's theory," I said gently, "is certainly all wrong."

"Geoffrey is a painter." Anne's voice was at its hardest, but I could see that her lips were trembling. "All this domestic mess he leaves to me. I assure you"—she turned to Appleby with something of her habitual serious mockery—"he would never shoot anyone unless I told him to. And Wilfred, as Basil ought to know, is a person whom . . . whom I have always rather liked. "Even"—her face became suddenly a child's—"even if he is a mean and tantalising old pig."

"May I ask—" began Leader, and stopped. Anne had burst into tears.

CHAPTER XXII

This was the point at which Lucy Chigwidden confessed. She stood up and said in a loud voice: "I confess."

Appleby looked at the clock and I wondered if the extraordinary entertainment we were putting up was beginning to bore him. It was he, however, who took charge of Lucy—and indeed from now onwards he was to bear a more active part in the proceedings. "Madam," he said gravely, "do I understand that you confess to the attempted murder of your nephew, Wilfred Foxcroft?"

"Yes," said Lucy firmly—and added a moment later: "No."

"No?"

"No—not of my nephew. Of my brother. I tried to murder Basil. Twice." Lucy looked round the room, as if to command all our attention. "Twice," she repeated emphatically.

Mervyn Wale put on his glasses and studied Lucy across the room, much as if he were meditating calling in Beevor once more. Ralph Cambrell, who was sitting disregarded in a corner, began to fiddle with his hat as if he would much like to clap it on his head and escape. Horace Cudbird was fidgeting too; I was increasingly sure that he felt himself to have something really decisive stored up. At the Voice I did not venture to look, but I have no doubt whatever that he was repressing his emotions only with considerable effort.

And now Lucy rose and walked slowly across the room to Anne and Geoffrey. She laid a protective hand on the shoulder of each. "In this monstrous charge against these poor lambs," she said, "one vital point has been overlooked: the attack on Basil just before all this discussion began. If they succeeded in what they planned against Wilfred last night, why should they turn and attack Basil this morning?" Lucy looked at us vaguely, as if trying to recapture the thread of her remarks. "But, as I say, I confess." She began to hunt about her chair for her hand-bag, as if the matter were now settled and we might disperse. Suddenly a thought seemed to strike her. "The motive," she said; "I quite forgot the motive. I hate Basil. Intensely. I have hated him from the nursery. The motive is that." She rummaged anew.

Appleby leant forward. "A motive is always useful," he said gravely. "But could you let us have a little evidence as well?"

"Evidence?" Lucy looked most surprised. "But I *confess*."

"My dear Mrs. Chigwidden, I am afraid that your confession, however vigorous, will never get you convicted. Evidence of some sort there must be."

"Lucy, my dear"—Hubert Roper spoke for the first time—"don't look so put out. We will all think you up some evidence if you want it. And what about this? Wilfred was most inefficiently shot. It is increasingly clear that the major puzzle of the affair is in that. If one wants to kill a man one goes for his head or his heart. Yet this shot, fired at a few paces, gets Wilfred in the right side." Hubert paused and looked round the room. "Now, could anyone except Lucy make quite such a muddle? Who hasn't seen her dip her pen in the cream jug and put sugar in her soup? Isn't she the only person one can imagine as getting things exactly the wrong way round—mistaking one man for another and his right side for his left?" Hubert turned to Appleby. "Search no further," he said lazily. "You've got your man."

I suppose Lucy's performance may be said to have done credit to her motherly heart. In the abstract world which she largely inhabited tears were no doubt a symbol of guilt, and she had accepted Anne's in that sense. Her attempted confession, however, had a woolly quality which I found irritating—though not so irritating as Hubert's trivial and untimely embroidery upon the mystery. With Hubert—and for reasons which must presently appear—I felt really angry. So did Horace Cudbird.

Cudbird stood up. "I am going to explain," he said, "what happened last night."

Out of the corner of my eye I saw the Voice muttering urgently to Leader. He may have been insisting—very reasonably—that in point of explanations we had already reached *l'embarras de richesses*. His expostulations, however, ceased abruptly: I imagine at some sign from Appleby. Cudbird was allowed to proceed. But not before Anne, whose power of recovery from emotion was rapid, had re-established herself as ironic chorus.

"A little bird has told Mr. Cudbird all about it. Doubtless a canary."

Cudbird nodded his head emphatically. "Yes, the canaries have had a hand in it, I don't deny. But for studying their ways I doubt whether I should have hit on the truth. Or but for that and an awakening interest in art."

"New interests everywhere." Automatically, Geoffrey chimed in on Anne's note. "Has everyone heard of Cecil gathering rosebuds while he might? One wonders if Rose fell."

With considerable presence of mind the Voice bent a severe eye upon the constable who was inclined to snigger. For a moment Geoffrey's joke hung uncomfortably in the air and then Cudbird went on.

"The trouble clearly starts with Sir Basil's proposal to sell Belrive and put most of the proceeds into an expensive expedition. A good many people might be worried by that." Cudbird paused. He was speaking with a deliberation that accorded impressively with a natural weight in the man. I felt my heart beating faster; I was convinced that he really had something to say. "A good many people might be worried. Quite suddenly, and as the result of what might very well appear a whim, a sizeable fortune is going—as somebody put it—to be fired at the moon. Or, at any rate, to melt away in the blizzard and the snow."

Appleby, who had been staring into the fire, transferred his gaze to the ceiling.

"Mr. Roper, here"—and Cudbird nodded curtly at Hubert—"might be worried. He is the heir. I don't suppose he would lose every expectation under Sir Basil's proposed dispositions. But certainly he would lose a good deal—including the actual estate, to which he may very well be more attached than his brother."

Appleby lowered his eye, caught my own, and nodded gravely. Then he returned to the contemplation of the plaster above his head.

"Mr. Roper might be worried, one can clearly see. And now about my canaries." Cudbird squared his shiny jacket on his shoulders and swept the room with his oddly compelling eye; he enjoyed this abrupt transition. "There are times when one of the creatures has to be put in a cage by itself. And often, poor thing, it is inclined to mope. . . . And now, I am afraid, I must get a bit personal. I want you all to take a look at Sir Basil, there."

We looked at Basil, wondering what connection might exist between him and the moping canary. It afforded me some satisfaction to see that Appleby was looking frankly puzzled.

"There's a resemblance—a family likeness—between Sir Basil and his nephews, Cecil and Wilfred. That I've already remarked to some of you here. But it's not a strong resemblance. Wilfred, from what I saw of him, is uncommonly like Cecil; the two of them are—though less markedly—like Sir Basil. It would be easier to take Wilfred for Cecil or Cecil for Wilfred than it would be to take either for Sir Basil." Cudbird paused to let this sink in. "And now let me recall something that Mr. Roper said a few minutes back. He said that Mrs. Chigwidden here is the only person one can imagine as getting things exactly the wrong way round. But that's just what the canary can do when you give it a bit of mirror."

Cudbird had made his effect. Hubert jerked suddenly upright in his seat, his laziness or affectation of laziness gone. The rest of us stared in fascination at the little brewer.

"When the bird is lonesome I've tried sometimes giving it a piece of mirror for companionship's sake. Two things happen. It pays a great deal of attention to the mirror. And it gets thoroughly confused. These two things are just what Mr. Roper has been doing."

"That," said Hubert Roper, "is true."

"Look at his sketches. They are obviously the work of months. And they are all taken up with mirrors: one mirror, two mirrors, three mirrors—even four. Sketches of the reflection of a reflection—a fascinating technical exercise I don't doubt."

I remembered that odd scene between Hubert and Geoffrey when Geoffrey had offered advice on the composition of Cecil's picture. Hubert had said something about slaving at just such sketches till he felt like Alice in the looking-glass. In this particular at least there was no doubt that Cudbird was on the spot. And there was a deadly effectiveness in the way he was developing his thought. It made everything that we had heard so far appear the merest beating in the air.

"You see the relevance of this to the grand puzzle in the whole affair: the fact that Wilfred Foxcroft was shot through the right lung. Work with an artist's intense concentration day after day at these tricks of reflection and you may very well find yourself thoroughly confused in a crisis. Constantly you have been putting on paper or canvas a left which you know is a right or a right which you know is a left. And then you step up to a brightly lit window and try to get a man in the heart. If you get his right lung instead—well, I for one won't be surprised."

"Nor I." Hubert was pale, but he was looking at Cudbird steadily enough. "I doubt if I've heard anything more plausible in my life."

"But that's not all. I have said that Cecil and Wilfred are alike, and that each bears a less marked resemblance to Sir Basil. Here we have something else that fits. Wilfred is shot; Wilfred is like Cecil; Mr. Roper has been studying Cecil—*in a mirror*. Now, there is a curious fact about human physiognomy—I think that's the word—which may be studied with the aid of photographic negatives. It is the fact of the asymmetrical nature of the human face. Take a photograph full-face and cut the negative vertically through nose and chin. You can then print three distinct faces: the normal one, using the two halves; a face made of the left side used twice; a face made of the right side used twice. But the relevant point here is one that I have learnt once more from the canaries. It is this. Asymmetrical characters may be inherited in a transferred position. And there is a particular sort of family likeness—the so-called 'baffling' sort—which is the result of this. If you will think for a minute you will see what follows. *The resemblance between two such people will become closer if one is viewed in a mirror.*" Cudbird paused. "And it will become less close again if a second mirror is introduced. Mr. Roper, then, trying out now one system of mirrors and now another for his

portrait of Cecil, is intensively studying an appearance
which is now more and now less like Sir Basil. And as
Wilfred is so like Cecil, the effect would be just the
same had it been Wilfred whom he was painting. I think
I need hardly labour the point of how confusing all
this is."

Leader, who had got tied up in a forlorn endeavour to
transfer Cudbird's reasoning to his notebook, nodded emphatically. Appleby had put his hands in his trouser
pockets; I remembered his bet with Cudbird and found
myself expecting him to produce five shillings there and
then. He did no more, however, than ask a question.

"Would it really work that way? You imply that the
shot was not fired at an unidentifiable figure simply because that figure was at Sir Basil's desk; it was fired because the features of Wilfred Foxcroft—no doubt briefly
and imperfectly glimpsed—were mistaken for those of
Sir Basil. Surely a painter, however bemused by this mirror business, would be the last man to fall into such an
error?"

I breathed more freely—but only for a moment. Cudbird shook his head. "Not *this* painter. There is nothing
that more bores Mr. Roper than the human face. He even
declares that there is only a handful of human faces ex-
tant. He has had to make too much bread and butter out
of them, and he dislikes them."

Hubert looked up and nodded. "Again," he said, "only
too true. I wish I liked the human race; I wish I liked its
silly face. But I don't." He regarded Cudbird with a
gloomy calm which alarmed me.

"Why all this business of mirrors at all?" Cudbird went

inexorably on his way. "Simply so that he can pretend to be painting faces when he is really painting other things. Technical things. Edges, for example—whatever they may be. You might say that Mr. Roper is obstinately determined that faces—unlike bricks, apparently—are all alike. And on top of that comes the fact that the actual faces involved have been approximating to each other in the way I have explained. There's no getting away from it. Hubert Roper is the man."

"Hubert Roper is the man." It was Hubert himself who spoke. He glanced at Lucy. "And he may as well confess at once."

It was a twist too much to some screw which had steadily been boring into my mind during this protracted and extraordinary scene. Something snapped. I sprang to my feet. "Stop!" I cried. "Hubert, for heaven's sake stop. I will tell them. . . . I will tell them who did it."

CHAPTER XXIII

I LOOKED round the library. "Cambrell," I said. "Cambrell did it."

My own voice came to me strangely. I had not meant to make this accusation, and I admit that I would not have made it now had I believed that there was evidence sufficiently strong to secure a conviction. But Hubert's danger—and I felt that the ingenuity of Cudbird made his danger very real—had roused me and I spoke on the spur of the moment. Doubtless Hubert's own wilfulness was finally responsible. I can see now that he had no intention of confessing to the crime. His words had merely been an ironic echo of Lucy's. But for a moment they had clouded my judgment and it seemed to me that if disaster were to be avoided the case against Cambrell must be vigorously put.

"Cudbird's construction is extraordinarily ingenious. But it is by no means the only case that can be built up to take account of the peculiar manner in which Wilfred was shot. The case against Cambrell, though equally surprising, is simpler and even more convincing."

I had been holding Hubert fixed with my eye. Now I paused, fairly well pleased with the manner in which I had modified my first outburst.

Cambrell took advantage of the silence. "I protest!" he said loudly. "I protest against the scandalous irregularity of these proceedings. If Roper here were not virtually incapacitated"—and he waved his hand at Basil—"he would not permit it for a moment. The chief constable shall hear of it. And who the devil is Ferryman to accuse me of criminal behaviour? If the police wish to interrogate me let them say so and I shall send for my solicitor. I came back here as a matter of courtesy. I will not stop to be insulted."

And Cambrell stood up as if to go. His attitude, if intemperately expressed, could scarcely be termed unreasonable. It was Appleby who intervened. Appleby had interrupted his contemplation of the ceiling when I had first spoken, and had looked at me with all the appearance of a man who expects the truth to emerge at last. But now the ceiling had claimed him again. He spoke almost absently. "I think," he said, "that Mr. Ferryman spoke at first in some excitement. From what he now says one gathers that he is not putting forward a charge. All this is exploratory—exploratory merely."

Leader gave a supporting nod. "We are exploring every avenue," he said sententiously. "Nothing more than that."

"We must leave," said Appleby, "no stone unturned."

"Routine," said the Voice. "Hearing the views of those concerned. Mere routine."

What these remarks lacked in cogency they made up for in confidence. Cambrell subsided beneath the soothing chorus. "Very well," he said; "I submit. Talk away. But I will not answer questions."

I took a long breath. "Cambrell wants to buy Belrive. So does Cudbird. I have reason to know—I fear it is something I overheard—that Cambrell offered the higher figure. Basil refused it; he preferred that Cudbird should have the estate for a lesser sum because he was interested in what Cudbird proposed to do. Cambrell was exceedingly angry. And he seems to have believed—this is again what I overheard—that Hubert, were he the owner of the estate, would be differently disposed. He believed that Hubert would sell—and sell to him. And we know, of course, that if Basil died Hubert would inherit the estate and have the power to dispose of it."

Anne interrupted. "But, Uncle Arthur, would a man, would an industrialist"—she looked at Cambrell—"would a *respectable* industrialist really take a gun as a means of possessing himself of land for darker and more satanic mills? As a motive isn't that a bit steep?"

"Not with Cambrell." I am afraid I was beginning to get some enjoyment from my thesis. "His mills bound his entire mental horizon. He thinks in terms of nothing else. What another man might do for a woman, or a treasure, he would do for his business. And you must remember that in this matter Cambrell has been in direct competition with Cudbird. A purely human element enters there. I believe he would feel a direct defeat by Cudbird as intolerable. Consider all this and the motive becomes a very likely one."

I paused to collect my thoughts. "Now, we know that Cambrell was actually in Basil's study last night. That is a matter of his own confession. But of a confession which was by no means voluntary. He left—and the mistake, as being evidence of haste, is significant in itself—a book of his own and took away one of Cecil's instead—Law's *Serious Call*."

Sir Mervyn Wale, who had been sitting huddled and silent in a large chair by the fire, endeavoured to interrupt upon this. "Speaking of that, I ought to say—"

But I was too wound up to pause. "He says that he came in by the front door, went directly to the study, found it deserted, decided that he had acted injudiciously, and retreated as he came. I find this not very easy to believe. Consider the book. Cambrell enters the study and finds it empty; he waits for a few moments and then leaves. Is it likely that in this slightly uneasy position he would set down a book he was carrying? But only if he had set it down would it be possible for him to take away another book by mistake. One can, on the other hand, envisage certain circumstances in which he *would* set down his book."

I saw Appleby nod slightly, and felt he approved the reasoning so far as it went. "And now I come to something which I *saw*. As I have told the police, when I went out for a stroll I saw the figure of a man lurking on the terrace. Would this not be Cambrell, waiting to catch Basil? He says that after having left somewhat angrily earlier in the day he felt some awkwardness in presenting himself again so soon to Basil's servants. If that were so would he not be more likely to slip along the terrace and walk into the study direct? You may well feel it to be inherently probable that Cambrell both came and went that way.

"With what intentions he would come one does not know. But if what I say is correct it is fairly clear that he did not actually enter the study until after the firing of the shot. It seems likely that he walked about in irresolution, or hurried away to get a weapon, and thus failed to mark Basil's leaving the room and Wilfred's entering. When he fired it was from behind the curtain; until he got his man he would not want to risk being identified. And *then*, when Wilfred fell, he would enter the room to make sure. He would kneel by the body—and this is the moment at which he would set down his book. He would find that he had shot not Basil but Wilfred, and that Wilfred was not dead. His one instinct would then be to get clear. He would snatch at his book —or at what he thought was his book—and depart as he had come. And he is a resolute man. What he failed to achieve in the study last night he attempted again in the ruins this morning—and that even after the police had traced something of his yesterday's movements."

I sat back in my chair in what would have been silence but for the sudden scream of Cambrell's siren calling his operatives back to work. It was far past lunch time. And now Cambrell again made a grab at his hat. "If you think," he said brusquely, "that you are at all likely to gaol me on the strength of *that*—"

"Not at all." I spoke with vigour. "Nobody expects anything of the kind. I am merely showing that you are as convincing a suspect as is Hubert."

Leader laid his pencil on the table before him and shook his head. "I don't know that you can be said to have done that, sir. Mr. Cudbird offered us a really clever explanation of the great puzzle: the odd way Mr. Foxcroft was shot. Whereas—"

"Whereas," interrupted Cambrell, "if Ferryman had at all attended to the revolver-practice yesterday he would have noticed that, of a good many good shots, I am myself by some way the best. If I wanted to put a bullet in a man at less than half a dozen paces you may be sure it would go just where I aimed it."

"And that is exactly what it did."

I think everybody in the library jumped. I had been saving up my last shot—which was a long one—for the most effective moment.

"That is exactly what it did." I looked deliberately round the room. "We have heard several explanations of why Wilfred was shot in the right side: because Lucy doesn't know her right from her left; because Geoffrey didn't want to kill his victim outright; because Hubert had muddled himself with his mirrors. But now I am going to suggest to you why Cambrell, capital shot though he is, shot Wilfred—or Basil, as he thought—where he did. The explanation is at once simpler and more surprising than any of the others. Cambrell and Basil are old acquaintances; they have scrambled about together on the Cumberland and Westmoreland fells."

Basil raised his head and looked at me in astonishment. The deliberate inconsequence I had achieved was less exquisite than that of Cudbird's in the matter of the canaries, but it must have been equally disconcerting.

"And on one particular occasion they had a misadventure. Basil—who was already something of a crack climber—took a tumble on a simple scramble and lay unconscious for some time. Cambrell had to stand by until help came. Now, what would be one of his first actions in such a situation?" I paused and then answered my own question. "He would want to assure himself that

Basil had not been killed. He would feel his heart. *And I suggest that he found it in the wrong place.*"

Once more Appleby nodded. And Wale in his chair by the fire stirred sharply and turned to look at Basil as if for the first time.

"There is a condition—it is, of course, rare—known as complete dextrocardia: Sir Mervyn will correct me if I am wrong. It is much as if what Cudbird has been pointing to in the matter of mirrors took place actually in the human body. *The heart is located on the right side.* If you knew of the existence of such a condition in a man and wanted to shoot that man dead *you would aim at his right breast.*"

There was a long silence. Then Appleby spoke. "Capital," he said. "The case couldn't be better." He shook his head regretfully. "Only it happens not to be true. Sir Basil is not dextrocardiac."

I looked at him in astonishment. "However do you know that?"

Appleby smiled engagingly round the company. "Because," he said, "I knocked him unconscious to find out."

It was the sensation of the day. People stood up; there were exclamations and cries; Leader could be heard gasping; the Voice turned pale with suppressed emotion.

"Of course," said Appleby mildly, "not as a police officer. As an acquaintance merely." He looked at his watch. "And our meeting had better adjourn."

CHAPTER XXIV

A LIGHT wind blew little flecks of soot across the surface of the snow. From behind a broken wall a piece of waxed paper fluttered; a hand followed, grabbed, crumpled it tidily, withdrew. I rounded the corner and came upon John Appleby. He was seated on a stone coffin eating a ham sandwich. Beside him on the ground was one of those flat bottles commonly used to carry spirits. It contained milk.

"I am glad to see," I said, "that you have had the grace to make yourself scarce. But perhaps you have merely come to gloat on the scene of your exploit."

Appleby merely took a large bite from his sandwich.

"I am inclined to think that you must be mad. Mad" —I added—"as the mist and snow."

"My dear Ferryman, we have found that you are inclined to think all sorts of improbable things. But, as you say: mist and snow." Appleby looked at the remains of his sandwich for a moment with quite a troubled face. "So much ingenious talk! If only"—he spoke in a sort of ingenuous reverie—"I could find the truth." Suddenly he looked at me sharply. "The truth," he repeated almost appealingly.

I said nothing. He unscrewed the top of his bottle and drank. "Yes, so much ingenious talk: it convinces me more than ever of that something which is altogether missing from our affair. . . . You think me mad? What

216

about Sir Basil—is he annoyed?"

"You might rather ask if he is furious. But he is not. I remarked to him that you might surely have asked him about his heart in a confidential way. He said that he could conceive reasons for your not doing so. Incidentally, he ate a normal luncheon and seems virtually recovered."

"Recovered! Of course he is. One has to learn to do these things efficiently." Appleby finished his milk. "And I certainly had my reasons. For one thing I wanted to get you all going. You helped me there, I think, by retailing our proceedings of last night: that rattled them a bit in itself." He chuckled shamelessly. "But an additional jolt was all to the good. Not that the main point lay in that."

"I should hope it lay in nothing so wanton."

"Ah. Well, you see, it was like this. The dextrocardiac idea struck me quite early on."

"Indeed." I spoke rather coldly. "I don't remember your mentioning it."

Appleby chuckled again. "Some ideas are so extravagant that one does best to keep them quiet. Still, it had to be tested. Wilfred Foxcroft hadn't a heart of that sort: we should have heard of it from the hospital. But perhaps Sir Basil had, and Wilfred had been shot in the right side by someone thinking he was getting Sir Basil's heart: your theory, in short. But then again perhaps *someone else* had. Perhaps Wilfred was mistaken for *someone else* with a dextrocardiac condition. In that case it would be conceivable that Sir Basil was the assailant. Because of that possibility I didn't want to give away my awareness of the dextrocardiac notion to him or to anyone else. Hence the method I employed. Of course when you aired the notion yourself concealment was no longer useful." Appleby suddenly sighed. "Incidentally, I made a mistake—a thing which in my profession one just can't afford to do. Sir Basil's shirt and waistcoat."

"His shirt and waistcoat?"

"I left them unbuttoned after feeling his heart. A small thing, Ferryman, but a mistake nevertheless." He screwed up the bottle and slipped it in his pocket. "Something missing." He pronounced this refrain flatly. "If I may say so, I am never more aware of it than when talking to you."

I was startled. "You have a weakness for enigmas, Appleby. I fail to follow you."

"I can't retort the charge. Your exposition of the case against Cambrell was most lucid. But I don't know that you at all believed in it."

I was silent.

"Or that you mightn't usefully have given us a little less theory and a little more fact. . . . I was interested in the moment you chose to break out."

From beyond the boundary wall of Belrive came the advancing clatter and clang of a decrepit tram. The uproar grew, passed, diminished and faded; it was a quiet hour on the main road. The unusual silence had the effect of making me feel it necessary to say something. "I was impressed by Cudbird's performance. He has an inborn rhetorical skill that I envy. Once he starts you can't get your attention away. It's like being buttonholed by the Ancient Mariner."

"Yes." Appleby's eyes had rounded slightly. He transferred their gaze to a cranny at his feet where the sun had begun to melt the sullied snow. "There was a moment when I felt almost persuaded that I had lost five shillings. . . . By the way, why did you come out to hunt for me in this way? Just to tell me that I am mad?"

I shook my head. "Perhaps a growing morbid interest. You lounge about disclaiming anything in the nature of action only a few minutes after hitting Basil hard on the head."

Appleby stood up. "I promise to do no more lounging about. We must be getting back. All those people are due to meet again at half-past two. And then I shall finish this thing off."

"Finish it off!" I cried. "You are in a position to do that?"

"Most decidedly." Appleby hesitated, and it struck me that he was about to make an important decision. "I know who fired that shot. I know whom it was fired at." He began to walk rapidly towards the house. "Geoffrey Roper spoke of a big black van. Well—it will be here in half an hour."

We walked for a time without speaking. Only a few minutes before Appleby had been confessing that the truth eluded him. How he could have received sudden illumination in the interval I found myself unable to imagine. But he had spoken with the greatest confidence and finality; indeed there had been something quietly ruthless in his manner of announcing that he was in a position to bring a criminal to book.

Despite myself, I felt extremely agitated. "You know,"

I said presently, "the prospect of a scandalous exposure in our family distresses me very much. That one of us should actually attempt the murder of a kinsman, perhaps of a near relation—"

"Quite so. Your attempt to present an academic case against Cambrell showed how you feel. But don't worry."

I stopped in my tracks. "I don't understand—"

"I said not to worry." Appleby spoke a shade shortly. "This is not a family affair."

"You mean that no member of our family is responsible?"

"Just that."

I stared at him, completely puzzled. I had never expected the problem to take this turn.

"So you see," he said drily, "you may feel relieved."

The police sergeant was poking about the terrace; he hailed Appleby with something like urgency. I lingered while they talked briefly together, and presently Appleby came back to me with a grave face. "I wonder," he said, "if you would go to the library and tell them I shall be a little late? I have some telephoning to do."

I looked at him curiously. His manner was almost normal; nevertheless it was just possible to perceive that he was concealing a good deal of distress. "Is it anything serious?" I asked.

He hesitated. Then he spoke abruptly. "Yes—serious and curiously unpleasant." He turned away.

I went into the house. It was a quarter past two and for some minutes I wandered uneasily about. In the dining-room I came upon Hubert who had lingered be-

hind the rest and now appeared lost in the gloomy con-
templation of a Stilton cheese. He looked up moodily.
"That fellow Cudbird," he said. "A smart little tyke.
Gave me a bit of a jolt."

"I can well believe it."

Hubert's glance returned to the cheese; it was faintly
puzzled. "Arthur—" he began, and paused. When he went
on it was to say: "And now he offers me a commission:
what do you think of that?"

"I think it in very poor taste."

Hubert ceased to look puzzled and looked very surprised instead. "What an extraordinary notion! I shall
never begin to understand you literary people. I think
: · grand. I'm to paint every slum in the town, brick
by brick. Years of real work. No more of those bottoms
masquerading as—"

"Well," I said, "if you think it grand I shall not dispute the point. But the police haven't taken to Cudbird's
idea of the shooting. At least you've had a narrow escape
and may be thankful."

"Oh, come." Hubert was beginning to show that bore-
dom which anything like sustained conversation always
induced in him. "It would have fallen to the ground
sooner or later, whatever the tiresome bobbies chose to
take to. A rigmarole like that."

"You never know. Further evidence might emerge."

Hubert pushed the cheese away as if it were important that he should be able to study the table-cloth beneath. "Do you know," he said slowly, "I believe I know
who fired that shot?"

I must have given a startled exclamation, for Hubert

shook his head almost reassuringly.

"No—I'm not going to air yet another theory to the world at large. Like you, I don't think any good would come of it. So far, all that talk has got the enquiry nowhere. Which is just as it should be. Let it remain so and presently the police will drift away and the thing will be forgotten about. As far as I can see"—and Hubert looked as if he were making an unusual effort at logical thought—"there will be no occasion for another attack. The motive has evaporated."

We looked at one another in silence. "Yes," I said presently. "That is what I have been thinking. Only there has been a fresh development. Appleby has announced that the mystery is solved. In a few minutes we are going to gather to hear the solution. What does that mean?"

"It means"—and Hubert smiled lazily—"that the guilty party had better go while the going is good. What does one get for attempted homicide? Something considerable."

"But that is not all. Appleby tells me that we need not concern ourselves. The family, I mean. It is not a family affair."

Hubert looked at me rather blankly. "He must be barking after Cambrell still. Even though Basil's heart is in the right place"—Hubert chuckled—"as I've always been brotherly enough to believe. Plenty of evidence still, no doubt, to build up a case on. For instance, one might combine your idea about his motive with Geoffrey's of firing backwards so as not to be recognized. Something of that sort. Poor old Cambrell." Hubert appeared vaguely amused.

Sudden extreme irritation possessed me. "I doubt," I said angrily, "if you even see the point."

"The point? My dear Arthur, I leave that to you."

Hubert got up, stretched out a long arm for a crumb of cheese on the table-cloth, and moved towards the door. I remembered the message with which Appleby had charged me and followed him out of the room.

The study door was open and as we passed we saw Appleby standing at the telephone. He gestured to us to wait and then spoke into the machine.

"Disgraceful," he said coldly. "The man's condition was known. You were told to follow him *closely*. And when the thing happens your fellow is twenty yards away. The result is this horrible business and an immensely more difficult case in court. I can't congratulate you. Good-morning."

He put down the receiver sharply and came to the door. "I shall come along with you," he said sombrely. "I'm through with that."

He strode down the corridor and we followed him wondering.

CHAPTER XXV

NEITHER LEADER, the Voice, the sergeant, nor the constable was in evidence in the library; I had the impression that the whole local police force was in disgrace. And Appleby had quietly but firmly assumed complete authority over all of us in the room. The atmosphere was wholly different from that of the earlier meeting during which each of us had been so fully given his head.

"Mr. Foxcroft," said Appleby without preliminaries, "was shot with a cupro-nickel jacketed bullet of .35 calibre; it was almost certainly fired, therefore, from an automatic pistol. That pistol I want."

Nobody spoke.

"At least one of you here knows its whereabouts. I appeal to that person to produce it. And to tell what he or she knows. We may thereby be saved a laborious and unpleasant investigation."

Again there was silence. Appleby was standing before a large window and we were seated in an irregular semicircle round him. He could not have placed himself in a more commanding position. Wale was directly before him, with Hubert on his right. I had myself taken a chair near the door.

"I am sorry that there is no response." Appleby looked momentarily troubled, as if doubtful how best to proceed. "I had hoped to get the shooting elucidated before having to tell you of something which I fear will be a great shock to you all. It concerns Dr. Cecil Foxcroft. I deeply regret to have to tell you that he is dead."

There was a little gasp of horror; then a chilled silence; and then Lucy Chigwidden began to sob. Basil crossed the room and sat down beside her. Some of us murmured to one another the mechanical and inadequate phrases which such sudden intelligence as this evokes. And then Appleby spoke again.

"Sir Mervyn"—he had moved quite close to Wale—"had you reason to apprehend anything of the sort?"

Wale shook his head. He was perfectly impassive and composed. "Your question is an ambiguous one. But, however interpreted, the answer is no. Foxcroft's physical condition was not such that I should have had any fear of his sudden death. And if you mean that he has taken his own life—again it is unexpected. His recent experiences had certainly upset his mental balance; as you know, I endeavoured to have him examined by a colleague this morning, and was prevented by his sudden departure. But I should certainly not have expected his distresses to take a suicidal turn. This is a great and unexpected misfortune." And Wale looked round at Cecil's bereaved relatives in the most placid way. "A vigorous and useful life. It is very sad—very sad indeed." He settled back comfortably in his chair.

"Dr. Foxcroft," continued Appleby, "had a luncheon appointment with a Mr. Podman, the father of one of his pupils. This appointment he kept. After leaving Belrive in the abrupt way he did he went, it appears, straight to Riverton and found Mr. Podman in his office. It was too early for luncheon, and so Podman offered to show

Dr. Foxcroft over his works. It is a big concern, and given over chiefly to making motor-car bodies. It was while they were inspecting some process connected with this that the accident occurred. Dr. Foxcroft must still have been in an exceedingly nervous condition, for it appears that for anyone exercising normal care the machinery is absolutely safe. Be that as it may, something happened to startle him, he stepped back hastily, tripped and fell. The machinery was halted at once, but it was too late. He was killed instantaneously."

Lucy had stopped sobbing, but now Anne had begun. It was against the background of her desperately suppressed sniffs that Wale spoke again. "It is a comfort," he said, "to know that he can have experienced only a moment's pain." He nodded his head in a satisfied way and gave a sad and resigned smile which was clearly meant to indicate what should be the correct family attitude. "May I ask"—he turned to Appleby—"where, for the moment, they have taken the body?"

Appleby looked extremely distressed. "And now," he said, "if I may suggest—"

But Wale insisted. "The body—where have they taken it?"

"I am afraid—it is a horrible thing to have to explain—well, I understand it hasn't yet been scraped off."

We looked at him appalled.

"Dr. Foxcroft fell into a very powerful press, used for stamping out steel bodies. He was instantly crushed. Not to mince matters, the remains can be no more than a few millimetres thick."

Our horrified silence was suddenly rent by a yell of

mingled despair and rage. It came from the hitherto professionally callous Wale. He had sprang to his feet as if
possessed and was waving his arms in maniacal fury.
Then, as suddenly, he collapsed.

And Appleby was on his feet in turn and pointing.
"There," he said dramatically, "is the man." His finger
was directed straight at Wale's heart.

I must have been almost stunned; I remember Appleby's voice coming as if out of a mist a few minutes later.
He was speaking rapidly and with extraordinary energy.
The absent and occasionally rather diffident young man
was gone. I suppose it was during this performance that
we all came to realise just how formidable a police officer
Basil had brought accidentally beneath his roof.

". . . and you have seen him give himself away. What
he worked for, what he almost killed another man for,
is gone—irrevocably.

"Has any of you read a story of Saroyan's called
Aspirin Is a Member of the NRA? An ironical sentence
in it has stuck in my mind. *Death does not harm the
heart . . . doctors everywhere recommend it.*" Appleby paused. "Death does not harm the heart—that is
what Wale wanted to ensure."

I remember a fleeting glimpse of astounded faces, their
gaze riveted on Appleby.

"Wale had to have Cecil Foxcroft's heart. He had to
have it; he is, as you know, a cardiac specialist, and it
had come to be his master interest."

Again a feeling something like giddiness came over
me. I recalled—I believe I have set down the fact earlier

in this narrative—that Cecil had possessed some sort of odd heart as a schoolboy. I recalled—more powerfully —the strangeness I had felt in the relationship between Cecil and Wale. I recalled—most vividly of all—that interview or consultation I had stumbled upon in the ruins, and the expression on Wale's face at its termination. That expression had elusively reminded me of something at the time: I now knew what it was. It was the same expression I had seen on the face of a collector in a sales-room when a rival had carried off a unique book he could never hope to see again.

"But Wale was by a long way the older man—and a sick man at that. He realised that in the normal course of things Dr. Foxcroft would cheat him—would cheat his passionate desire to possess and investigate something of unique scientific interest. I believe he realised this particularly keenly during a game of which Mr. Ferryman has told me. You were searching for bells in Shakespeare and had collected rather a melancholy crop. When it came to Wale's turn—or to one of his turns—he quoted from *Romeo and Juliet*. He quoted: *This sight of death is as a bell That warns my old age to a sepulchre*. And then he left the room in some agitation. He knew that he had not very long to live and that Dr. Foxcroft was unlikely to predecease him." Suddenly Appleby wheeled on Wale. "Is that not true?"

Wale was lying back in his chair, pale and exhausted. He nodded. "Yes, it is true. But—"

"He determined to kill Dr. Foxcroft, but in such a way that the organ he coveted should not be injured. He found a simple plan to lure his victim to the chosen

place. Dr. Foxcroft had mislaid a book: William Law's
Serious Call. Wale found it. He placed it in the study
and told Dr. Foxcroft that he had seen it there. He so
arranged it as to reckon on Dr. Foxcroft's going to
retrieve it after he had changed and just before dinner. Unfortunately Dr. Foxcroft"—Appleby hesitated—
"found something else to occupy him. And by a further
stroke of ill luck Wilfred Foxcroft—who has been remarked as uncommonly like his brother—entered the
study instead. The rest explains itself. But there remains
the curious manner in which Dr. Foxcroft hit upon the
truth.

"It happened when Wale came back from the hospital after Wilfred Foxcroft had been operated upon.
Dr. Foxcroft was in the hall and asked for news of his
brother. By a very odd chance the terms in which Wale
briefly replied almost brought together the words 'serious' and 'call.' And at once Dr. Foxcroft's mind leapt
to the truth of what had happened. Wale was his physician and the one man who understood his condition;
he depended on him absolutely. But this must have made
him all the more aware—subconsciously at least—of the
extraordinary species of covetousness with which Wale
regarded his supremely interesting patient. And now the
truth leapt up: the information about Law's book being
in the study had been given for a profoundly sinister
purpose. Perhaps Dr. Foxcroft had already been suspicious; perhaps Wale had been clumsy in giving the information. Be that as it may, Dr. Foxcroft suddenly saw
his physician transformed into a Shylock of a peculiarly
horrible sort, eager not for a pound of flesh but for

several pounds of human heart.

"I do not think it disrespectful to the late Dr. Fox-croft to say that he was not a courageous man. The circumstances were unnerving to an extreme, and he is not to be blamed if he lost his head. His one idea was to preserve himself from Wale. He hit upon what must be admitted an ingenious plan. He sent for a solicitor and proposed to make a will—or something between a will and a manifesto, for the document was to be made public immediately. However he should come to die—this was in effect his wish—there was not in any circumstance to be a post-mortem examination. If he could achieve this, and Wale were to know it, he would be safe. When he was assured by the solicitor that he had no power to make a legally binding disposition of the sort he abruptly left Belrive—with the unhappy result that you now know.

"All this might be difficult to substantiate. But, as it happens, Dr. Foxcroft set down most of what I have told you in a document written early this morning, and this document he gave to Mr. Cotton, the solicitor, with in-structions that it should be transmitted to the police in the event of his death." Appleby paused for a moment and then turned to Wale, who was still sitting huddled in his chair. "Sir Mervyn Wale, I arrest you—"

"Stop!"

The voice had rung through the room. It was my own.

"Stop, I say! This perversion of justice—this mon-strous ingenuity—it must not go on. I have withheld the truth too long. Hubert shot Wilfred. That is the truth and I have known it from the start."

Hubert looked up as I pronounced the last words,

and I saw that his face wore its laziest smile. "I didn't expect this," he said. He sighed and the smile vanished. "It was Arthur. Arthur was the fool who did it. And now the police must know."

CHAPTER XXVI

APPLEBY glanced from one to the other of us. "Mr. Ferryman," he said gravely.

I looked steadily at Hubert. "You will all realise that I didn't mean to do this. When Cudbird produced his penetrating explanation of why Hubert shot Wilfred as he did I intervened with a case against Cambrell. I hope Cambrell will forgive me. Hubert seemed about to confess and I rushed in with the first diversion I could think of. For I was desperately anxious that Hubert should not be publicly convicted of his horrible act. It was a momentary madness, I felt sure, and best forgotten. I tried to get from Hubert in a veiled way an assurance that he could be trusted not to act in so wicked and foolish a way again. His response was not very satisfactory; he is a wilful creature; still, I felt the slight risk had better be borne than that the family should have to figure in a criminal court.

"But then there came this sudden and frightful complication. The police, who had appeared baffled amid a welter of our conflicting theories, hit on one of their own: this diabolically clever construction of Mr. Appleby's against Wale. Before we resumed this strange conference after luncheon Mr. Appleby told me that he had a case, and that it concerned none of us in the family. I told Hubert of this at once: the imminent prospect of some positive miscarriage of justice clearly presented both of us with a formidable moral problem. But his attitude was again very unsatisfactory. He implied that any problem was wholly mine. It must be supposed that he was already preparing the fantastic accusation against me which he made a minute ago.

"And now there is nothing for it but the truth. I don't know how many actual lies I have told; I think not many. What I have done is to suppress something vital."

Appleby had once more taken up his position before the window. Now he interrupted me. "The gun," he said. "You can produce that?"

I nodded and moved to the door. "In less than a minute." And I went out into the hall. "I hid it," I explained on my return, "in one of those Egyptian pots. It startled me rather to find poor Cecil poking about them in his inquisitive way later last night. Here it is." And I laid the gun before Appleby.

He looked at it thoughtfully for a few moments. "As I thought," he said. "An automatic pistol. Will you all excuse me?" And leaving the weapon on a table beside him he rose and left the room.

It was an uncomfortable interval. We all looked at the gun; we none of us looked at each other. But after a minute's silence Hubert spoke. "Arthur, why didn't you beat it when he let you out of the room? You don't think this yarn of yours is going to be any good?"

I did not reply. The silence prolonged itself. Appleby, by disappearing in this unexpected manner, had hung up my statement in the most awkward way. And it must have been a full eight minutes before he reappeared. "Go on," he said.

"I was saying that with the object of protecting Hubert I had suppressed something vital."

Hubert stirred in his chair. "Would it be interrupting too rudely," he asked, "if I returned the compliment? I had no wish to see Arthur in gaol. So I said nothing about seeing him come out of the study and slink away with that gun. If that isn't vital, what is?"

There was a murmur of bewilderment. Geoffrey Roper, who had been uncommonly subdued since his performance before luncheon, turned to his father. "I say, Dad, aren't you going for something a bit steep? I don't see what motive Arthur could have—"

Hubert shook his head. "There have been some imaginative motives flying about. But not the authentic imaginative motive. Whenever any of you claims that Basil was to be shot because of his proposing to sell Belrive the motive is given in terms of pounds, shillings and pence. But can't you see another? Poor old Arthur is crazy about the Priory, and always has been. He lives in the past. He would do anything to prevent the place from being broken up. And he guessed that if Belrive came to me there would be no sale. Rather a compliment that, considering that I never have a bean. So I'm sorry, as I say, to have to give him away. But when he tries to plant the thing on me—"

Appleby interrupted firmly. "I think we had better begin with the vital matter which Mr. Ferryman says he concealed."

I nodded and braced myself. "It is this. Before dinner, as everyone knows, I went out for a stroll. I saw somebody on the terrace: I had to admit that to Mr. Appleby, being taken rather by surprise. Let me try to remember just what account I gave of myself. I was down by the lily pond when a flash from a tram showed me this figure. I think I said I waited for another flash which didn't come. That is true. Then I said that a few minutes later I turned away from the house and entered the park. That again is true. What I suppressed was something that I did in those few minutes.

"I was curious and for some reason slightly alarmed. I retraced my path, climbed the steps and moved along the terrace. There was a chink of light from the study window and by this I could just see that the figure was Hubert's. He was standing right back by the balustrade, where he could not be recognised or distinguished from within, and he was gazing intently into the room. He moved slightly and I saw that he had a gun."

Hubert stood up. "That," he said—and I knew that for the first time he was angry—"is a lie."

I turned to him. "Do you deny that you were there?"

"I was there—and I was a fool not to admit it to the police at the start. No doubt I was staring in intently. I have the habit of staring intently: it is part of my job and a lighted window can be a fascinating thing. But that I had a gun is a lie."

"Go on," said Appleby.

"Very well." I thought for a moment. "It may sound strange, but I persuaded myself that nothing was wrong. Or rather I must instantly have forbidden myself to believe that anything could be seriously wrong. I had an idea that some foolish joke was going forward—a mock-hold-up or something of the sort. These parties are occasionally high-spirited. But certainly I didn't want to be involved in any foolery of the kind, and I turned away. But this blanketing of the sinister quality of what I had stumbled upon did not last for long. I walked about, increasingly uneasy, and finally I returned to the terrace near the study window. Hubert had disappeared, but the pistol was there still, lying on the balustrade. In something like sudden panic I picked it up, stepped through the window, parted the curtains and walked into the room. I saw the body huddled on the floor and in an instant saw the truth. Hubert had shot his brother Basil —whether fatally or not I could not tell. My one instinct was to avoid a scandal if that might be. I ran out to the terrace, pocketed the pistol and hurried round to the front door. It was my intention to go straight to the study and appear to come upon the disaster for the first time. But my plan was upset by the appearance of Mr. Appleby and I had to dissimulate my alarm. The news that it was Wilfred who had been shot dumbfounded me. But I was committed to concealing Hubert's ineffective crime."

Appleby turned to Hubert. "And you saw Mr. Ferryman come out of the study with the pistol. Between your stories there is, in fact, only one discrepancy. Mr. Ferryman says that when he first recognised you you were carrying the pistol. Now—"

"Not carrying it," I interrupted. "That is inaccurate. He had laid it on the balustrade just by his hand."

"You mean"—Appleby's voice was particularly calm—"you simply saw it *lying on the balustrade?* Mr. Roper was standing by the balustrade and facing the window, and the pistol was on the balustrade—close to, but not actually in, his hand?"

"Yes."

Appleby stood up. "Our investigation," he said formally, "is concluded."

Tea had been brought in. There were stacks of muffins. Appleby's appetite proved to be considerable.

"It was fortunate," he said, "that Dr. Foxcroft's nerves gave way and that he came to cherish such extraordinary apprehensions about Sir Mervyn. That enabled me to give Ferryman—who is a most unusually obstinate person—the final jolt. And it is fortunate, of course, that Dr. Foxcroft himself is alive and well. He will no doubt quickly recover nervous tone."

"Cecil is alive?" Lucy Chigwidden, although she had received this good news several times, seemed too bewildered to take it in.

"Certainly. Sir Mervyn—who most assuredly has the passionate interest I ascribed to him—may have his chance yet. And, as I say, I let case after case be built up in the hope that it would produce the truth—and the pistol. I was almost certain that it was Ferryman who was concealing something. When we met on the doorstep, and before he ought to have known that anything was wrong, he struck me as a man endeavouring rapidly to conceal some perturbation or other. In my job one develops a nose for that sort of thing."

"You also develop," said Basil drily, "remarkable muscular control." He touched his bandaged head tenderly.

"And you may also think that we develop distress-

ingly thick skins. But I thrust myself forward as I did
because I feared that my colleagues here might make only
too efficient an attempted murder out of the mystery.
That explanation I was myself reluctant to accept from
the first. As you all assembled in the hall after the shooting I began to form an impression which was never seriously modified subsequently. I do not know that you
are a very amiable household, but I do know that you
are not the sort of household in which homicide crop
up. That was what was so pervasively absent from the
case: the atmosphere, the particular sort of tension which
generates itself around a murder. You are, if I may say
so, a theoretical and talkative lot, happy to sit about and
accuse each other of the most extraordinary ingenuities
But you lack the passion to kill. Even Miss Anne"—Appleby smiled—"Miss Anne whom I like the best of you—
even she would use only impalpable daggers."

Geoffrey Roper disengaged himself from a muffin and
looked childishly pleased. "Uncommonly lucky," he
said, "that a person of your penetration should happen
along."

Appleby rose and handed his cup to Lucy for more
tea. "Of course," he continued as she hunted for the
cream jug, "less indefinite factors pointed to the likeli-
hood of accident. The entire household had been engaged
in revolver-shooting. The injured man fancied himself
as both a theoretical and practical gunsmith—"

"Verona drops," I said.

Appleby smiled. "The drops exist—but are they *Verona* drops? I rather think not—and that is all to the
point. Wilfred Foxcroft has a great deal of information

and much of it slightly muddled. His technical dexterity is no doubt in the same case.

"Then there was the gun. The bullet, when recovered, proved to be jacketed—and that meant an automatic pistol. Such a weapon is always more dangerous than a revolver, for when the magazine is removed a live round is usually left in the chamber. It is because of this that such weapons commonly have a thoroughly effective type of safety catch. This particular pistol"—and Appleby picked up the weapon I had so disastrously concealed—"normally has that. A grip lever is fitted at the back of the stock, so that the hammer and sear are disconnected unless the weapon is actually being grasped by the hand. But the designer didn't reckon with the mechanical curiosities of Wilfred Foxcroft. He had emptied the magazine, quite failing to remember the round left ready to fire. And then he had fiddled. He had fiddled out there on the terrace. And then—growing bored, no doubt—he tossed the pistol upon the balustrade and abandoned it. It lay there—about the next best thing that could be devised to a deliberate infernal machine.

"It lay there while Hubert Roper was strolling on the terrace; it lay there close to his hand as he stood and gazed into the study. It lay there, in fact, until Ferryman, having formed his not unnatural false conclusion, picked it up to conceal it. And its final mischievous appearance was in Ferryman's hand as Roper came back from his stroll and observed it."

"But meanwhile," said Basil, "it had gone off."

"Meanwhile it had gone off. And that was the puzzle. Or rather the second puzzle. For me, clinging to the theory of accident, the first puzzle was the absence of a weapon. I put its disappearance down to some officious act"—Appleby glanced at me ironically—"and then this second puzzle remained. Accidents commonly happen when a gun is in somebody's hands, or is otherwise in movement. But if that were not the case—if this were an accident about which nobody knew—how could the thing have happened? The pistol could not have been on the desk: there would have been scorching had that been so. In fact it could *only* have been out on the balustrade —the shot passing through the open window and the chink left in the curtains by Wilfred Foxcroft. But if that were so how had it gone off? For, however perilous the equilibrium in which the mechanism had been left, *some* positive agency would be necessary. I thought of, and experimented with, various things: a trail of ivy, a blown leaf. Nothing answered. And all the time—infuriatingly—I knew that I had the explanation somewhere in my head."

"Mist and snow," I said.

"Exactly. Sir Mervyn, returning from the hospital said something about mist and snow. That made me think of a poem, a poem in which lay the solution. It eluded me until someone made another chance remark. Ferryman said something about Cudbird being like the Ancient Mariner. It was Coleridge's *Ancient Mariner* that was lurking in my mind. Or rather just two lines of it. *And now there came both mist and snow, And it grew wondrous cold*. The solution lay there. *And it grew wondrous cold*. That, you will remember, is just what happened last night. And it was the cold, ever so slightly contracting the metal of the pistol in the perilous state Foxcroft had left it, that caused the tail of the trigger to slip from the bent of the hammer and so to fire the round. It was all as simple as that."

Appleby stood up. "Wilfred Foxcroft is on the road to recovery. When I left the room a little time ago it was to ring up the hospital. He has been able to answer one question. They asked him if he remembered leaving a pistol out on the terrace. He replied that he did.

"So the Belrive mystery has been what I always hoped it would be—a case of Much Ado about Nothing. Only for Dr. Foxcroft I fear it was for a time—well, a Comedy of Terrors." And Appleby advanced upon Basil much as he might have done the night before had our dinner party gone as it was planned. "I hope you will forgive me that hard knock. And that your expedition to the mist and snow will be a success. Good-bye."

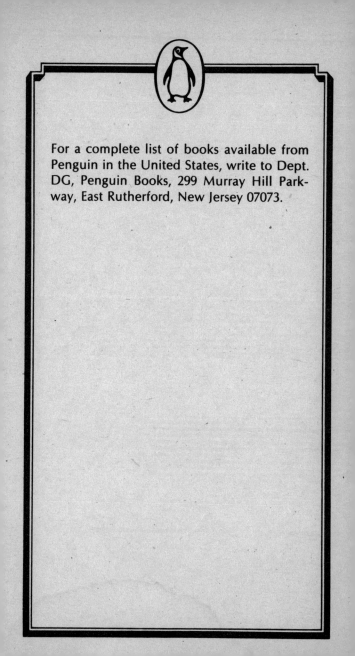